THE VAMPIRE STORIES

OF

Ñancy Kilpatrick

THE VAMPIRE STORIES

OF

Nancy Kilpatrick

mosaic press
CANADA

Canadian Cataloguing in Publication Data

Kilpatrick, Nancy
   The vampire stories of Nancy Kilpatrick

ISBN 0-88962-726-6

I. Title

PS8571.I493V36 2000   C813'.54   C00-931083-5
PR9199.3.K54V36 2000

Published by MOSAIC PRESS, P.O. Box 1032, Oakville, Ontario, L6J 5E9, Canada. Offices and warehouse at 1252 Speers Road, Units #1&2, Oakville, Ontario, L6L 5N9, Canada and Mosaic Press, 4500 Witmer Industrial Estates, PMB 145, Niagara Falls, NY 14305-1386

Mosaic Press acknowledges the assistance of the Canada Council, the Ontario Arts Council and the Department of Canadian Heritage, Government of Canada for their support of our publishing programme.

MOSAIC PRESS, in Canada:
1252 Speers Road, Units #1 & 2,
Oakville, Ontario, L6L 5N9
Phone / Fax: 905-825-2130
ORDERS & SERVICE:
mosaicpress@on.aibn.com
EDITORIAL:
cp507@freenet.toronto.on.ca

MOSAIC PRESS, in the USA:
4500 Witmer Industrial Estates
PMB 145, Niagara Falls,
NY 14305-1386 Tel:1-800-387-8992
ORDERS & SERVICE:
mosaicpress@on.aibn.com
EDITORIAL:
cp507@freenet.toronto.on.ca

Le Conseil des Arts | The Canada Council
du Canada | for the Arts

Acknowledgements

I must always acknowledge the very special people who have endured in my life, making this strange, exciting, horrifying journey more than bearable: Stephen Jones, Eric Kauppinen, Mike Kilpatrick, Mitch Krol, Sephera Giron, Michael Rowe, Mandy Slater, Caro Soles, Mari Anne Werier, and my special companion Hugues Leblanc. I also want to thank Howard Aster for his generosity of spirit which allowed room for this work. And then there's my darling Bella, in all her strange manifestations.

– Nancy Kilpatrick

Table of Contents

THEATRICAL VAMPIRES

Passion Play 3
Theater of Cruelty 20
Metadrama 33

EROTIC BLOODSUCKERS

Dark Seduction 45
The Game 62
The Hungry Living Dead 70
Vampire Lovers 77

MYTHOLOGICAL
& HISTORICAL REVENANTS

In Memory of... 89
Memories of el Dia de los Muertos 101
The Mountain Waits 104

BATS WITH BITE

The Shaft 113
Teaserama 116
Virtual Unreality 123

THE UNQUIET UNDEAD

Farm Wife 135
Root Cellar 140
UV 146
Sustenance 154
I Am No Longer 160
Leesville, LA 165

Nancy Kilpatrick

An Appreciation

Nancy Kilpatrick, like J. G. Ballard, makes mosaics. Her stories are rarely entirely linear and do not depend on the usual elements of horror fiction, often the result of too much movie-going, of building to a single shocking/disgusting surprise. There are no exploding heads or sanguinary swarms of Bad Guys in any guise coming in waves of rising devastation. There is also no sentimental twaddle to excuse cruelty. That is not the way she tells a tale: instead of these rather commonplace devices, Nancy Kilpatrick assembles a display of elements and insights which, when completed, imply as much beyond the resolution of the plots as they reveal about the events depicted.

This is crucial to good horror story-telling, for if too much is revealed, the horror is lost. After all, the reader thinks, it is only a vampire. All I have to do is get a stake and some garlic and Bob's your uncle. But when more is implied than shown, then the horror takes on the element of the unknown that leaves a lasting impression in the mind of the reader, and the niggling suspicion that it *might* be something more than your garden-variety vampire, or ghoul, or other mainstay of horror literature. And worse than any outside monster, the object of the horror might be . . . *you.*

In this collection Nancy Kilpatrick shows a number of creepy sleights-of-hand that leave the reader with the uneasy feeling that the solution to the conflict in the story might be more complex than it seemed at first, that the issues are larger than the confines of the tale being told. She is able to imbue her resolutions with a kind of unease that lends itself to the various, low-level anxieties that bedevil us all, creating a quality of potential that can lead to anything from failed relationships to natural catastrophes. It is the *aftermath* of her stories that give them their special kick, the way in which the ripples flow out from the conclusion of the story that make the images linger and grow. It is her ability to present these implications that sets her work apart from many of the other writers in the field and gives her such a distinctive voice.

Creating this aggregate of images is trickier than it looks, and Nancy Kilpatrick makes it look very easy. Her eye for the telling detail is always sharp and her ability to select the single most cogent element of an image is spot-on. She is also sensitive to the charaters' role in these illuminating moments: she presents their perceptions as part of the whole, giving a kaleidoscopic view of the events rather in the way Impressionistic painting evokes a range of responses in the viewer. She does not rely on cinematic frights and starts – futile on the page in any case – nor does she go in for *Gotterdamerung* endings that drag all the 20th century down in flames. Nancy Kilpatrick knows that great secret of horror stories: that they are intensely personal. The End of the World is a great E-ride concept – unless it is happening to you. These stories have scope, but that scope is always anchored in the immediately personal, in the myriad, personal experiences that lead to the experience of horror.

Each story in this excellent collection brings a new angle on her insights, particularly her more extended work. She has an evolving concept of horror and here she shows the fruits of her contemplation. She is keenly aware that horror is a very delicate flower, needing a careful touch to be sustained. She is not given to bludgeoning the reader with heavy-handed gore or filling the pages with exploitive rape-fantasies or so-called philosophizing. Her social resonances are just that: resonances. As an example of this, her take on the interplay of horror literature and the Goth movement is intriguing, and unobtrusively presented. She raises the question of the source of horror: is it inward or outward, self-generated or imposed externally created? Since one of my greatest annoyances in introductions is having the point of the stories explained to me before I can read them and find out for myself, I will not comment on individual works. But I will point out that much of Nancy Kilpatrick's story-telling contains a sly commentary with the human fascination with danger and the darker aspects of human nature. In addition, I will recommend that you do not gobble these tales whole, but that you give yourself time to explore each one to the fullest, getting full literary nourishment from the menu she has provided. This is haute cuisine, not barbecue, and deserves your literary gustatory respect.

– Chelsea Quinn Yarbro

Foreword

A few thoughts from Nancy Kilpatrick

Over the years I've had so many requests for some of these out-of-print vampire stories that it made sense to do a collection. I've always wanted to publish a book in Canada, and am delighted that Howard Aster, through Mosaic Press, opened a window of opportunity.

Vampires to me are complicated beings. They have evolved from the simple disinterred corpse, back from the dead, hell-bent on revenge. Vampires, in the last century, came into their own. Now, they reflect back the dark-side of humanity, the nasty bits we have ignored or hidden from, swept under the proverbial carpet. The parts we like to pretend do not exist. It's always been my belief that if we as a species do not integrate or in some manner reconnect with our shadowy selves, we have sealed our own doom, and have only ourselves to blame. I see the vampire as reflector of our dark desires: for passion, longevity, power, creativity, control. They are much like us. At their worst, they personify human fears, madness, evil. At their best, they are seekers of truth, struggling with meaning in an age where the meaning of life must be found, as Joseph Campbell told us, in the value we give to every moment.

I hope these stories will move you in some way. I also hope you'll find them a fine read. But in all good conscience I feel compelled to offer a few words of warning. Especially when dealing with vampires, it's always prudent to remember what some forgotten sage (paraphrased) said: if it doesn't kill you it just might cure you.

– Nancy Kilpatrick
Montreal, 2000

Theatrical Vampires

Passion Play

—◦—

"I'm looking for a man."

Neanderthal eyebrows lifted. "You're in the right place, babe."

Sweat-scent rode the smoke and Cheryl found herself sucking straw-size breaths through her mouth. "His name's Nightshade."

The bartender paused a heartbeat. Green cone shades illuminated the felt on each of the dozen pool tables—islands of light amid the dense gloom. He nodded to the furthest corner.

As she walked that way, Cheryl felt eyes like laser beams scan her body, stopping in places of preference—her high-thigh skirt, the short red t-shirt. No one said a word; they didn't have to. She wasn't unfamiliar with this macho world, although she never felt completely comfortable in places like this. She always felt alone.

A game was underway in the corner. While one man leaned over the table, another seven clung to the darkness near the wall. A stack of paper money balanced precariously on the edge of the pool table.

The sandy-haired man was just about to make a shot when Cheryl's heels stopped clacking on the hardwood. He turned as if the silence was noise, said "Fuck!", dusted his cue tip with blue chalk angrily and assumed a classic pool-player's stance. His cue pushed forward and struck the white ball too hard, at the wrong angle. The ball spun crazily and dropped into a pocket. He sent a murderous look in Cheryl's direction as he retreated to the wall. She folded her arms across her chest, feeling both guilty and defensive.

Someone materialized out of the shadows. Tall. Lean. Long hair tied back, as black as the eight ball. His dark denim jeans and open black leather jacket fit his form like skin on a snake. A silver cross

3

earring glinted in one lobe. She saw letters down the front of the midnight t-shirt:

A

B

O

AB

Universal Recipient

Dramatic, she thought, then modified her judgement. Melodrama.

He stalked the table, circling it twice with sexual grace, eventually stopping at a corner so that he faced her directly. All eyes were on him. In fact, most of the room had paused to watch. He lay the cue ball behind and to the right of the head spot then dusted his cue slowly, the motion sensuous. He leaned low across the felt, the leather of his jacket crackling softly. The light brought out a translucent quality of his flesh; shadows highlighted his cheekbones and a strong chin. A handsome corpse, she though, and he flinched slightly as if he'd read her mind.

He made a bridge with his right hand and lay the stick across it. Cheryl noticed the handle. Mother of pearl inlays glittered beneath the yellow bulb. From everything Aleron had told her, that was just his style.

The shot was a perfect set up. Cue ball. Eight ball. Cheryl's groin. He hunkered down behind the white, eyes close to the felt, and adjusted his bridge unnecessarily, going for drama again. She watched the cue ease back, the tip aim at the bottom of the white. The air cleared and the space between the two of them hollowed into a tunnel where time hovered.

Suddenly his head shot up. Yellow eyes soldered into her green ones. Eyes the color of flowering Buffalo-bur—the Nightshade family. He winked at her at the same time his lips twisted cynically downward. Mesmerized by his stare, she heard more than saw the cue slide as if in slow motion. The cue ball started forward fast then suddenly stopped dead in its tracks. It shifted direction and spun under itself across the table. White barely tapped black. Black rolled willingly into the hungry mouth waiting to devour it.

Reality fractured as if one of the green glass shades had crashed to the floor and shattered. Noise. Movement. Balls clinked, smoke clotted the air. He was already unscrewing his cue, returning the two halves to the case, pocketing the money. Walking past her.

"Nightshade!" she called sharply.

He stopped but did not turn.

She watched his broad shoulders tense as she said, "Aleron sent me."

Now he turned, an animal focusing. A hungry animal. Ferocious. Before he could say or do anything, she said sternly, "My name is Cheryl. We need to talk. In private."

He handed over his case to the bartender in exchange for a key to a store room. Cheryl entered first and walked toward the antique pool table in the middle of the small room, surrounded by three walls of empty beer cases. When he was inside, he closed and locked the door.

"Turn on the light!" Cheryl said, feeling the threat of blackness.

Coming here, into his territory, wasn't such a good idea, she realized. Tense energy rushed toward her. She backed into the table, trying to avoid what she now realized was unavoidable, and braced for the inevitable. His powerful vibration overwhelmed her. In the darkness his lips barely brushed hers on their way to her throat. His incision was quick, precise, almost surgical. Painless. In no way dramatic. Obviously he wasn't the type to waste time when he was hungry, even if he had plenty of time to waste.

Cheryl felt energy drawn from her veins, sucked up through her heart and down from her head. Cold silver light exploded on the inside of her eyelids, freezing her thoughts. Her limbs went glacial and began to numb. She struggled to shove him away but he was stronger, as she knew he would be. He could leave her near death. Vulnerable. Or worse. "Stop!" she pleaded, but the word was almost inaudible.

Finally he did stop. Not when she asked, when he was ready. As he moved away, Cheryl's body collapsed onto the pool table, the weakened rind of a fruit after the pulpy juice has been sucked out.

More light flooded her brain, a myriad of stabbing colors. At first she though it was an hallucination from rapid blood depletion. But the faint chatter, the clink of ceramic balls striking one another told her he'd opened the door and she was losing him. "Wait! Please," she gasped.

He closed the door. He didn't have to. She knew that. His energy was still impatient and as bright as hers had become faded and dim.

Cheryl propped herself up and looked in his direction. She could not see him but knew he could now see her clearly in the dark. "I need help."

"Call a doctor."

"Aleron said I could trust you."

"Aleron lied."

"Before he died he told me where to find you. He said to tell you he's calling in his chips. You owe him. Pay me."

He was on her before her pulse could move along the small amount of blood remaining in her body. She suspected if there had been any blood left worth taking he would have yanked it from her veins and left her to the mercy of the mortals.

He grabbed her hair. His eyes glowed supernaturally, shooting yellow sparks at her in the darkness. His pale face flashed disbelief and pain. She knew he and Aleron had been close, once, and suddenly understood why.

Whatever his face betrayed, his words belied those feelings. "Were you a masochist before you died or did it come with the transformation?" He shoved her back against the table. She heard a click. White funnelled light from the shaded blub overhead rocked crazily around the room. Cheryl howled and covered her eyes against the solar-like glare.

"What did you expect?" he demanded. "I'd greet one of Aleron's castoffs with open arms? Welcome to my nightmare, sweet virgin of the dusk? I always wanted a child."

"Aleron said you can be cruel."

He laughed. The sound cut through her like a claw ripping its way down her backbone. "He should know." Teeth bared, he looked fierce. "He didn't teach you much about vampire etiquette before it bit it, did he? How unlike him not to foster independence. Maybe we should go nip Miss Manners."

He grabbed Cheryl and forced her to look at him. The power he emanated was horrifying and beautiful at the same time. "One, vampire baby: never, ever venture into the territory of another nosferatu. It's an act of aggression. What happens next is instinct. You just got a taste of mine as I got a taste of you. Got that?"

She nodded weakly.

"Two: we are a solitary species, in case Aleron didn't manage to convey that. If you should accidentally wander into another's designated dining area, get the hell out as fast as you can. Am I making myself clear?"

She nodded again.

He looked at her with a combination of revulsion, pity and annoyance, and pushed her away from him. "How long?"

Cheryl propped herself upright. Her head swam. "What?" She felt his impatience like an assault.

"What do you think I'm asking? How long have you been coming to pool halls?"

"I've been like this just over a week. Ten days."

"Damn!" He ran a hand through his hair. "Aleron was always a sucker, so to speak, for blondes. And brunettes. And redheads. So, why are you here?"

Cheryl crawled up onto the pool table so she could sit; she didn't have the strength to stand. She studied his vitality and wondered how he's react if she asked him for a little blood. Just to tide her over.

"Don't even think about it," he said.

"As I so obvious or can you read minds?" Her brain felt dried out and the room was weaving worse than the light. She bent her head, trying to keep from passing out, and fell forward. A hand like a wall held her up.

"I hope Aleron rots in hell!" she heard him say, accompanied by the muted sound of leather crackling.

The scent spread up through her nostrils and down her throat. Copper roses. She opened her eyes and saw a river of rubies. He pulled her head to a slit in his chest and her lips found the wound as easily as a nursing baby finds a nipple. She held his shoulders in a vice grip and sucked. Warmth flowed in, expanding out from her stomach and through her icy body, defrosting her. The metallic roses blossomed and warm rain coated her flesh. Warm rain in moonlight...

Suddenly she was cut off. It was as though a silver knife severed her into two sections—heart and head.

He shoved her away. "Greedy little leech. Don't expect to be invited back to any of my parties."

She felt much better. Mind clear, body energized. She was still hungry. He pressed two fingers to the wound near his heart and within seconds the bleeding ceased.

As he was slipping his t-shirt and jacket back on, she noticed defined muscles dancing beneath his skin. "Why'd you help me?" she asked.

He turned away.

"I mean, you could have left me here to rot. Aleron said you might."

He turned and the look on his face was amusement. "Aleron said that, did he?" He threw back his head, opened his mouth and roared with laughter—he looked like a wild animal so self-satisfied that for once it lets its guard down. His stained incisors glinted steel-strong and were longer than Aleron's. She felt in her own mouth with her tongue: her eye teeth would grow. Aleron assured her of that. In the mean-time, she'd have to find another way to pierce skin. If she could bring herself to do it. All the blood she'd drunk until now had come from Aleron.

Again, his words said he was privy to her thoughts. "I suppose Aleron fed you with an eye dropper." His eyes turned serious and one side of his mouth pulled back in disapproval. "As of this moment, vam-pire baby, consider yourself weaned. Tomorrow night you eat or starve."

The idea frightened her. She didn't know how to feed. Didn't know if she could even bring herself to do it. Drinking some blood from Aleron, and now Nightshade, was one thing. Taking it from a breathing, pulsing mortal... Someone who was very much alive as she herself had been not so long ago...

He reached out and instinctively she ducked, but he only pulled the cord and shut the light. He crossed the room, opened the door and was gone. Cheryl hesitated then jumped up to follow.

Nightshade had collected his case and was already starting down the steps to street level by the time she caught up. His hips held just the right amount of tension. His stride was long, his legs muscular and powerful in the tight black denim and she had trouble keeping pace. Aleron had told her that her strength would increase over the years. What he didn't tell her she had deduced: for a while—and she didn't know how long—she would be as fragile as eggshell, far more sensitive to impending daylight than he, more volatile in her needs. In fact, her hunger was outrageous by any standards she knew. She wanted food— no, blood—when she wanted it, and all other drives paled in the face of what she was quickly learning was a compulsion. Not one she had any control over either.

Nightshade stopped beside a black Jaguar with tinted windows. This is probably where he seduces his victims, she thought.

After they were both seated, he looked at her. "Better buckle up, darlin'. At least that's what I tell the warm-blooded men and women who usually sit in that seat."

Suddenly she was tired of being toyed with. "Look, if you can read my mind, just say so."

"Anybody can read your mind. Your heart's on your sleeve and your thoughts, mundane though they be, are imbedded in your pretty little face like gossip from *Variety*."

Despite the insult, she felt a secret thrill that he'd called her pretty. She stifled that thought, though, in case he was aware of it. "Where are we going."

"Nap time."

Annoyed with him, she stared straight ahead, not waiting to give him any satisfaction. Not wanting to give him anything. This old vampire, new vampire routine was growing stale. But even as she thought that, she also felt surrounded by liquid exhaustion, a feeling much the same as when she used to dive into a pool and be engulfed by water. Pressed from all sides. Weightless. Alone.

When Cheryl opened her eyes she was lying in darkness alone. She sat up and banged her skull against something solid. She felt above her and to the sides and realized she was in a wood box, a coffin. A panicked scream was just erupting from her gut when the ceiling raised and strong light poured in.

"Sleep well, my little seraphim?"

When she could tolerate the light enough to open her eyes, Nightshade's perfect features filled her range of vision.

"Let the hunt begin!" he said with a sonorous tone, walking away. Then, "Shake your booty, scream queen."

She sat up in what was a coffin-like box. It wasn't like any coffin she'd seen before, not that she'd seen many. Aleron hadn't slept in one, but he did require complete darkness. As did she. The rectangular box was big enough for two, and she was naked. "How'd I get here?"

"You metamorphosed into a bat and flew in your sleep." He stood, legs apart, hands on his slim hips, wearing a variation on yesterday's outfit, looking handsomely ferocious. "I carried you in from the car, how do you think?"

"You didn't sleep with me, did you?"

He raised an eyebrow, crossed his arms over his chest and made a disgusted noise. "Aren't we being just a tad precious, princess of darkness, not to mention unnecessarily chaste? And ungrateful. I don't have a spare casket. I wasn't expecting company until the millennium."

She hauled herself out of the box and onto a platform that took up most of the floor. Her clothes were next to the coffin. She felt his eyes licking her body and her nipples hardened; she dressed quickly.

The hardwood floor was a stage. A heavy scarlet curtain with big tassels along the hem hung at the edge of it, and beyond a domed ceiling littered with blazing stage lights. Out in the darkness she saw rows of ornate seats. Other than that, the relatively small space was bare. "This is a theater!" she said astonished, slipping her skirt up over her hips, remembering that Aleron told her Nightshade had been an actor, and a good one, at least before he changed.

"No kidding. All the world's a stage, honey, and the play's the thing. I am the star of this farce," he crossed one arm over his midriff, extended the other above his head and bowed deeply. His body snapped upright. "And you're the bit player."

"Why are you so hostile to me?" She turned on him, sick of his cynical jabs. Hunger made her irritable.

He walked to stage right and flipped a switch. The platform with the coffin on it lowered into the floor; wooden floorboards raised to disguise the opening. Another switch clicked and footlights caught her from below. She cringed to avoid the searing light.

"How did Aleron die?"

She'd been waiting for this question but now that he'd asked she didn't know where to begin. "It was out of the blue. Could you turn those lights off?"

"You mean it wasn't cancer? He didn't wither away? How odd." Nightshade stalked her. She was intimidated by that wave of power she'd felt the previous night. "Cut to the chase, honey. You might have all night, but I have plans to keep and miles to go before I sleep."

"There was a fire in my building during the day. The firemen came with their hoses, breaking down doors and windows..."

He turned and walked away from her, his cowboy boots slamming the boards.

"He died instantly. I don't think he suffered."

He spun back. "You don't think he suffered? How the hell would you know, you fledgling twit?"

"Look, don't take it out on me. I didn't start the fire. I would have saved him if I could."

Before she could blink, his face was in hers. "How come you survived? Aleron had two centuries of experience under his belt. Seems suspicious to me."

"You don't think I did that to him? What possible motive could I have? He was my protector. He helped me adjust."

"He brought you over. Was it against your will or did you grow up in the burbs loathing garlic and dying to sleep on dirt?" His face was cold, murderous. "How about revenge? You wouldn't be the first. Like I said, Aleron wore blinders."

"You hated him. Why do you care how he died?"

"I'm more interested in why you lived."

Cheryl was silent. She would never beat him in a word battle. Anything she said would be misinterpreted, twisted and used against her. Frustration mixed with vulnerability and she burst into tears. "I loved him. Maybe you can't remember love."

She sobbed into her palms, her body racked with the pain of loss. Cheryl had no idea she could feel so deeply about someone she'd known only a short while, but the bond was intense.

Through the agonized sounds that welled from her, she heard him say, "'Yes, I too can love.'"

She peeked through spread fingers. He was looking at her but his eyes were really inward, remembering, she suspected, people from his long past. Maybe remembering Aleron. His face had contorted into an agony that made her sadness seem like a shallow emotion. When he became aware of her close scrutiny, Nightshade's features altered like a shape shifter transmuting to a completely different form.

"Bram Stoker's *Dracula*. The infamous count's rebuttal to the three vindictive bitches of the night who are trying to justify their tryst with that cretin Jonathan Harker."

"Isn't anything important to you? Don't you take anything seriously?"

He cupped her chin and looked earnestly into her eyes. "The wine of life, my dear, a pleasing script and a gorgeous cadaver."

She shoved his hand away. "I'm hungry."

"I'm sure you are. And you'll eat. Once you explain why you, too, were not barbecued."

She sighed and looked around the stage, wishing for a chair. She wasn't physically tired, more emotionally drained from this roller-coaster ride. There was no chair in sight and she considered perching on the edge of the stage. But the lights were hotter there and, too, she decided any weakness she showed would be used against her.

"Aleron made me sleep in a huge trunk at the foot of the bed. He slept under the bed. He said my skin was too raw for even electric light."

"And why didn't the trunk incinerate?"

"It was cast iron. Aleron brought it with him. He said you gave it to him."

Emotion flickered in Nightshade's eyes and he turned away.

"Look," she said, "I know you and Aleron were close—"

"This isn't a B & B. Get out and get it before it's contaminated."

He headed out the stage door into the alley. Cheryl followed, feeling nervous. This was a test and she sensed it would not go well. Hunger swelled within her like a rush of sexual heat. She would not be able to resist and yet she couldn't see how she'd be able to kill a human being.

She hurried to keep abreast of him, asking, "Tell me about it. How do you do it?"

"Well, first you rent evening clothes—in your case a diaphanous gown—and a long cape. Next you practise a hypnotic stare. Just be careful you don't accidently put yourself under. Then—"

"Come on. I'm scared. I've never done this before."

He stopped under a street light and looked down at her. Something about what she said or her naivete must have touched him. She wondered if he was reminded of his own beginnings. Gently he brushed a lock of stray hair back from her forehead. His finger tips lingered on her skin. His eyes softened. "It takes getting used to. You don't have to hit the jugular; any old vein will do. Just make sure you avoid severing an artery or you'll have a body to dispose of. You don't have to kill them, you know. If you go to the right places, most will give you the blood willingly."

"They will?" She could hardly believe it.

"My dear, 'The only way to get rid of a temptation is to yield to it.' Oscar Wilde. *The Picture of Dorian Gray.*"

"Look, I know you don't have to help me. I just want you to know how much I appreciate –"

He cut her off by walking away.

They reached a basement club called *Necropolis*—dark and smoky with ear-splitting splatter rock and flashing lights. Everybody here looked like they'd just come off the set of a vampire movie. Nightshade moved through the crowd easily—it seemed to part dramatically to let him pass—and stopped at the chain-link bar.

A redhead with one side of her head shaved, wearing electric purple lamé tights under a black leather mini, and Doc Martens on her feet threw her arms around Nightshade's neck. He grasped her hips and whispered something in her cuffed ear. She looked Cheryl up and down, leaned over and yelled, "Hiya, I'm Poppy." Then she turned back to Nightshade and nodded. He slipped an arm around her waist and led her out of the club. Cheryl followed like a faithful puppy.

Within two blocks they reached a rundown brownstone. The girl seemed drunk or high. She giggled and swung her hips into Nightshade's all the way up the three flights of steps and ran a hand over his backside and between his legs. Inside the cramped apartment, she headed right for the cluttered bedroom, stripping her clothes from her body and kicking off her heavy boots. Nightshade followed, but didn't undress.

Cheryl looked around. Cheap fabric covered the lamp next to the double futon. A mishmash of items hung from the ceiling with no discernible theme: a mobile of hypodermic needles, a wind chime made of shotgun shell casings, an anatomically correct skeleton of a child— Cheryl hoped it was plastic. This girl could have a disease, she thought, scanning the filthy clothes and dirty dishes scattered around the room, not to mention the ferret skittering across the floor, wondering what, if anything, vampires are immune to. When she turned to the bed, Nightshade's face was between Poppy's legs. The redhead writhed and squirmed and groaned as if she was out of her mind yet managed to reach over and press a series of buttons on a CD player. Nine Inch Nails blasted from the speakers. Cheryl pressed her hands over her ears.

This was unbearable. She didn't have to put up with this. If Nightshade wanted to screw some crackhead, that was his business, but Cheryl had better things to do. Once she got away from this insidious noise, she'd be able to think what those things were. At least the music coated the acid jealousy searing her gut. She started toward the door.

An invisible beam galvanized her energy, forcing her to turn.

Poppy's hips rode the air, circling, pumping to the beat. Nightshade turned his head and grinned. His eyes blazed magnetic sunlight. But it was the crimson sunset smeared across his full lips and dripping down his long fangs that attracted her more.

Cheryl moved as if she were a hooked fish being reeled in. She crawled onto the bed. Poppy's nipples were hard pink nubs; Cheryl's mouth found one and pulled it up with her teeth. The girl groaned. Nightshade vacated his position and Cheryl moved down Poppy's taut flesh, past her naval to the red forest. Nightshade's incision still flowed just above the clitoris and Cheryl's lips sucked at the wound. Each mouthful of crimson fire plunged the girl into spasms of ecstasy and Cheryl drew fast and hard, feeling a flash fire spreading through her own genitals.

Suddenly she was yanked backwards across the room. "Bastard!" she shrieked. She tore at him, gouging his face, kicking, punching, tangling with him on the floor, spewing rage. How dare he keep her from that fire!

Nightshade was far stronger. He dragged her backwards out of the bedroom. Once they were beyond the prime scent range, he pinned her arms behind her and pulled her hair until her head was back and her throat exposed. His hot wet lips pressed onto her skin, close to her ear. "Chill, baby, or I take it out of you."

The idea of the blood leaving her body sobered her fast. She was panting, sweating, her body trembling uncontrollably. Finally she calmed enough that he relaxed his hold, then released her.

She gulped in air, trying to slow down and get a grip. Through blurred vision she watched Nightshade walk into the bedroom. Her perception was off; she couldn't tell if he's been gone a long time or a fraction of a second. When he came out she heard him say something like, "She'll be weak for a couple of days but no major damage. Beginner's luck, but you need discipline, young one, even if you are teething. Learn to restrain yourself or I'll restrain you, and if I do it, it won't be pretty."

On shaky legs she followed him onto the street. The night moved at triple speed and then there were moments when time stopped. She watched an old man in a doorway. He moved closer. Or did she move closer to him? His face lifted and his cheeks crinkled. She felt so linked with him. Soul connected. His eyes registered surprise. Pleasure. Fear. Suddenly Nightshade was by her side, scowling, tugging her away.

His hand on her bare arm felt wonderful. She turned and looked up at his seductive face. When those gold fire eyes met hers, sparks flickered between her legs; she wanted him.

They were at the theater. On the stage. He raised the coffin and opened the lid. "Get in."

Panic seized her. "Why? It's early. I'm not tired. I'm still hungry. I—"

He pulled her in with him and closed the lid. She felt them descend. "It's too dark. I'm afraid."

She heard a switch flicked and subdued light filled the sides of his satin-lined bed. His face, so near, so naturally necessary. Eyes like twin suns caught hers. "I'm hungry," she whispered again.

"I know."

Lips grabbed onto lips. His hand slid under her skirt, up inside her. Liquid broke over his fingers and her body quivered as she moaned. She licked his chest and stomach and his hardening penis. He squirmed as her mouth controlled him. She tensed her lips and his flesh grew taut, straining.

He undressed, her t-shirt came up, her skirt was kicked down around her ankles. She crawled on top of him, letting herself slide onto him until he was deep in her.

She propped herself up by her arms and arched her back as far as the confined space would permit. Her hips rode his. The folds inside her rippled and swelled with electrical tension. He nipped at her nipple in much the same way she had nipped at Poppy's and she moaned again, astonished at the spiralling pleasure.

The orgasm exploded through her like a dynamite charge. Shards of light sprayed past the edges of her skin, melding inner and outer realities. Her body went rigid before it went slack and she collapsed on top of him.

His was still firm inside her, his muscles tense, his eyes hungry for her. In one movement he flipped her over so that he was on top, thrusting deeper into her than he had been before. He bit into his wrist until the blood flowed then moved the wound to her mouth. Her lips found the red river and drank. His teeth found her jugular. He whispered,

"That was only the first act, sweet vampire baby. Stay awake for the finale."

When she woke the next night, Cheryl found a sprig of flowering Deadly Nightshade in her hand. Lighted votive candles in tall glasses lined the edge of the stage, casting a romantic Phantom-of-the-Opera-type glow over the shadowy space. The theater was empty—she could sense that now, or rather sense that Nightshade was not here. She was beginning to realize that the absence of living or undead defined what she experienced in the presence of both.

She felt incredible. Magnificent, really. Last night, when they made love, Nightshade had opened a new part of himself to her, as she had opened to him. He was vulnerable. Needy. He must have been alone for a very long time—Aleron said they hadn't been together for half a century. As strong as her bond with Aleron had been, her connection with Nightshade was more intense. Sharing their bodies in so many intimate ways—sharing the blood—it was a union she had not dreamed possible. Cheryl was startled by what she felt for him. The attachment ran deep and wide, as though they were soul mates, lost and wandering through time, who had found one another. And she was acutely aware of one other thing: blood was no longer her only obsession. She wanted sex. With Nightshade. And she wanted a lot of it.

She dressed quickly and waited, but when he didn't turn up and her stomach began cramping with cold as if she'd swallowed dozens of ice cubes, Cheryl made her way to *Necropolis*.

It was earlier than last night and the crowd thin. Nightshade was nowhere in sight and she was disappointed. She did, however, spot Poppy dancing with a large guy in ripped parachute pants and a chartreuse spiked cut. The girl looked pale but not much worse for wear. Before Cheryl could reach her, Nightshade appeared between them. Her body reacted like a plant moving toward the light. Every cell opened to receive him and a wave of lust nearly knocked her off her feet. When he took her arm and led her outside, she went willingly.

"I was just going to see how Poppy's doing..."

He pulled her up the street and into an alley. The pressure on her arm was beyond what was needed. "Don't be so rough." She jerked away. "What's with you? Last night you make love to me and now–"

"Make love? How pathetically romantic. I fucked you. We feed, we rut. A biological knee-jerk, that's all. Yours isn't exactly a warm body, but you were there."

She avoided his eyes, feeling cut to the marrow, thrust into an alien landscape, alone, and not wanting to expose that. "You arrogant bastard! I'd rather dehydrate than put up with your coldness one more night."

"Easily arranged."

"Aleron was a saint compared to you. No wonder he left you!"

The arrow hit the target; he looked wounded. Within seconds his face hardened. "I want the truth," he demanded.

"About what? I can't read your mind, remember?"

"What really happened to Saint Aleron."

"I told you."

He moved on her and she shouted, "Don't threaten me," but it didn't stop him from grabbing her by the throat and pressing her up against the rough brick wall.

"There have been no serious fires in this city in the last ten days."

They glared at one another for long moments. Finally he said, "You killed him, didn't you?"

"Yes," she whispered.

He let her go and, before she realized it, had disappeared.

Cheryl searched the streets, *Necropolis*, Poppy's apartment. She broke into the theater. Nightshade was not there. She knew he likely wouldn't be back; it was no longer safe.

Standing in the middle of the vacant stage, sensing him everywhere and yet not here, her heart felt empty. Again. The pain of losing Aleron was compounded more than she could imagine by the loss of Nightshade. In only one night he had fused with the deepest part of her and now, as with Aleron, she had been ripped in two. It was more than she could endure. Nightshade warned her they were a solitary species. She should have paid attention. Kept her heart locked away. A sudden terror of eternity spread out before her and the long and lonely road she would walk. It sent her out into the streets again.

Eventually, she found him in the pool room, dawn an hour away. She hadn't eaten and felt so weak and stiff her joints would barely function.

He was the only one left in the room, shooting balls in the corner alone. She dragged a bar stool across the floor and sat nearby but not too close. He didn't look at her or in any way acknowledge her presence until he paused and said, "'The weight of this sad time we must obey. Speak what we feel, not what we ought to say. The oldest hath borne most; we that are young, Shall never see so much, nor live so long.' *King Lear*. Do you know the tragedy?"

Nightshade reracked the balls. He bent low over the table and broke the triangle, sinking three balls at once, each in a separate pocket. "Aleron taught me to play the game. We came here together for nearly five years after he changed me. I think he stayed with me the longest. I didn't bore him as much as the others. At first. But, in the end, he always grew bored. He would have gotten bored with you too, eventually."

"He did," Cheryl said shakily.

He paused then continued around the table. The blue two ball, the red three, the purple four. Each remaining ball in numerical sequence found a pocket. When he sank the brown-and- white-striped fifteen, he started to rack them again.

"I killed him because I loved him too much." Her voice faltered more than she expected. She sighed heavily, feeling the weight of impending daylight pressing on her body and the dark emptiness descending into her soul. "I felt so sorry for him. He cried and cried; I didn't know what to do. He said he couldn't stand it any longer. Nothing engaged him. No one."

The memory of how Aleron had looked at her, his grey eyes pleading for something she could neither identify nor supply, struggling to find a reason in her and coming up empty. "He had me chain him on top of the bed and leave the curtains open. I slept in the trunk. I didn't really understand. The next night, when I got up..." Her body trembled. "There were only bones."

Tears streamed down her face. "He told me you loved him more than all the others he'd changed. That's why he sent me to you. He said you'd understand somebody who could love. Who needed love." Her body spasmed. The light was becoming scalding but she did not have the strength or the will to retreat to the cooler, darker shadows. Nightshade's eyes pulsed energy and strength and she wished she could draw some of it inside herself; she felt her own power ebbing.

She stood and walked away, unable to bear the ache of being near him. Maybe, if she could bring herself to face that ball of cleansing fire in the sky... Could there be salvation for the lost and lonely in annihilation?...

A voice filled the room. "'Oh mistress mine, where are you roaming?'"

Cheryl wasn't aware of movement, but Nightshade was suddenly before her. He cupped her chin and lifted her wet face.

"You loved him most," he said. "You gave him what he longed for, what the rest of us couldn't give him. What I couldn't give him."

His sun gold eyes seared away her loneliness. "You don't hate me?"

He kissed her lips tenderly then passionately. "Come home with me, vampire baby. I'll feed you and put you to bed. Tonight. Every night."

"Take me to bed," she corrected, throwing her arms around his neck.

He packed his cue into the case and, clinging to each other, they headed back to the theater.

Theater of Cruelty

"I want the original script. No last-minute rewrites," Nightshade said.

He and Cheryl sat on the edge of the stage, dangling their feet like children, cowboy-boot heels knocking the back boards, looking out at the non-existent audience. Her aventurine eyes stared straight ahead but her gaze was tuned to her private reality, as if waiting for an internal cue.

He caressed her chin with his index finger and forced her to face him. A copper chain holding a small copper ankh hung around her neck. She'd been wearing it the night she appeared at the pool hall two and a half weeks ago. Aleron's— a gift, no doubt. Nightshade restrained himself from ripping it from her throat.

He scanned her luscious features. They had fed early tonight; she no longer look deflated, although her eyes held a haunted quality.

Her full lips invited him. He leaned in and licked them. They parted the moment his tongue pressed for entrance. Her mouth tasted rich and meaty, the full flavor of blood still lingering. He moved a hand behind her neck. For a split second she resisted, then yielded as he pulled her tight against him. He wanted to devour her. He wanted to fuck her.

Mind censored instinct and he eased away. Her eyes fire danced. They beckoned him and to keep his body from responding more than it already was to the heat, Nightshade hopped down into the orchestra pit and moved quickly through it and up into the theater. When he reached row 'Q', he took the aisle seat, orchestra, center section.

The darkened house forced him to zero in on the bare, lit stage; a set would have been superfluous. She perched left of center as if a director with a sharp eye had carefully blocked this scene, placing her just so. Black backdrop, black floor boards, red velvet swaged curtain. Female lead costumed in a long slate leather skirt slit to the thigh, Harley-Davidson black jacket, black boots with silver stitching.

Even from here she was one of the most beautiful creatures he'd ever seen. And a natural on stage. The overhead lights accentuated the feminine contours of her face and body but drew the audience of one right to her large, tormented eyes. He wondered what she had looked like before the change. Did her hair glow as if a spotlight shone on it constantly, the light radiating from her to illuminate an entire theater? Had her body swayed and undulated with the small, precise movements of a trained actor who conveys so much with so little? Did her gestures come as easily to her then as they did now, taunting both men and women, teasing, promising to open with only a slight twist of her lips or arch of her brow? He decided she must have been much the same, otherwise Aleron wouldn't have noticed her. Aleron only plundered the best.

Nightshade turned in the seat to cross his long legs in the aisle. He leaned back against the red velvet, arms folded over his chest, the crackling of his leather jacket the only sound.

He could tell when she was lying. The light her body emitted flickered the way a spotlight does when the electrical current becomes sporadic. He hoped she wouldn't lie to him now. He wanted to trust her. He needed her more than she could understand. His existence had become repetitive, a one man eternal touring company, seven nights a week in a show that had long ago bombed. He'd been waiting for some new direction, a way to alter what felt like an endless performance before an audience too unsophisticated to appreciate his abilities. He needed someone to play off. A connection. He and Cheryl were so close to forming one. A part like this was rare and he was afraid he might blow it.

"Tell me about Aleron," he said gently.

She held her breath. Stage fright. She had forgotten her lines, or didn't know how to deliver them. Rehearsal was over and it was too late to run and hide. Suddenly she sighed. Her shoulders slumped from the pressure of being held rigid and her jaw relaxed a bit, making her face less mask-like.

"He'd been watching me," she said. "For a long time. I didn't know."

"Where did you meet him?"

"In, well, a kind of church. *Freewill* is different, though. It's New Age. Sort of a community. They're into wholeness, getting in touch with your helpers, with a higher power—"

"Ah, Janice."

"You know her?"

"She's one of us."

Cheryl looked startled. She caught the corner of her lower lip between her teeth and nodded. "I'd only gone there once before. I had no idea Aleron was even there. It's as if he was invisible or something. He was good at disguising himself."

Nightshade thought about the night he'd met Aleron. That chameleon quality struck him right away. Aleron could be whoever and whatever he wanted to be, or what you wanted him to be. Lover. Protector. Persecutor. But never your victim.

"...and that night, as I was walking to the bus stop, he drove up in a silver Fiat, the windows tinted like mirrors, and introduced himself. "'You left *Freewill*. Come in out of the rain. I can take you where you want to go.'

"I remember bending, to look through the rolled down passenger's window at him. Inside the car it was like a black hole, with only these grey eyes. They were the center of the universe and I felt dragged towards them, as if everything, as if I was compelled to revolve around them. I don't know what made me get in.

"I felt shivery. 'Can you turn on the heat?'

"'I will,' he said.

"He kept staring at me and again the omniscient power of those eyes hit me. You'll think I'm nuts, but it's as if they were made of grey glass. I mean, I could see through them. Inside I glimpsed snatches of a flat alien landscape, fascinating and horrifying. He made me so nervous I started babbling. Something like, 'So, do you go to the *Freewill* often? I've been there twice. It's an interesting place—'

"'Cheryl, I will visit your locked vaults and stroke the darkest contours of your soul.'

"I froze. What he said was so weird, but put so matter-of-factly.

Just another hustle, I told myself. But there was an undercurrent of demand... I don't know. Instead of telling him to fuck himself, or laughing it off, I blurted out, 'How do you know my name?'

"'Do not fear me. Destiny pulses and throbs with a tantalizing rhythm all its own. The most a mere mortal can do is adjust the volume. If destiny decides to play you as a passion song, you'd best dance to that melody of your own volition, sweet Cheryl, because whether or not you want to, you have drawn a partner, and you will be dancing.'

"'Listen, I think you'd better let me out...'

"He switched on the CD player. Haunting sounds burst through the car's interior from half a dozen speakers. The eerie acapella music violated every orifice of my body. I clamped my hands over my ears and practically curled into a ball, but the women's cries pricked at my pores like tiny insects determined to dig their way inside me. Within seconds every thought in my head had been annihilated. My body vibrated from note to note and became the chanting. I felt I didn't exist apart from those sounds. I became a cloud, formed, dissolved and reformed by fate, completely bound up with the fundamental essence of the universe.

"Suddenly the sound died. It was so abrupt I screamed. Silence crushed my eardrums. My clothes were soaked with sweat. My body trembled, way out of my control, assaulted in a different way because now that the music had stopped, I felt...empty.

"'Hildegarde of Binden, born in 1098,' he said. 'Abbess of a community of nuns attached to a Benedictine monastery; composer of contained ecstasy. Penetration by a Gregorian chant is not much different than being penetrated by a god. Have you not secretly wished to be impaled by a god?'

"He pushed the steering wheel up then slid over the gear shift, moving as smoothly as quicksilver. Before I could protest, he was on top of me and my seat was back. The car had stopped; nothing looked familiar. Only his grey eyes. When I looked into them I felt comforted and disturbed at the same time.

"But the darkness surrounding me was absorbing me. I was terrified but stunned. And when his grey eyes stared so intently into mine, all I could do was surrender to their transparent brilliance because they'd become the only things in the universe I could cling onto to keep from disappearing.

"'Feel how deeply I enter you,' he whispered. 'Learn and remember. You will pierce me as deeply, to my core. I've waited a long time for your light to burn through my darkness.'

"The strange chanting returned, capturing me, ravishing me, leaving my body—now naked—limp in his arms.

"His penis pressed hard against me, insistent. My thighs were slick with juices and they parted as if I couldn't control them, but I didn't want to control them. He thrust into me once, fast and deep. That movement was so serious and passionate. Fierce. My head fell back. I sobbed when his icy lips clamped onto my throat. Despite the chilly air that made me shiver, my blood boiled through my veins. That scorching heat ripped through me like a forest fire, consuming me as it ate my genitals.

"My hips bucked and writhed under his hard thrusts. The music took me up and his determined body dragged me back down to earth again. He controlled me completely. I felt caught in the jaws of pain and pleasure. My brain stopped sending messages, abandoning my body and soul to this dangerous ride on the edge of time and space. Exquisite explosions rocked me, one after the other, and they went on forever. I heard myself screaming in agony and ecstasy, wanting him to stop, to never stop. And all the while I knew the life was being sucked from my body and my soul was becoming chained to his. And I didn't care."

Nightshade was aware of a knot of tension in his shoulders and rotated his neck. Her elaborately told tale was too similar to his own. The seduction, the compulsion to give himself over to Aleron, a compulsion that soon turned into an obsession.

She was staring down at her folded hands.

"There's one line missing in that scene," he said.

Cheryl looked up. Even from here her eyes were red-rimmed. Blood-tinged tears stained her cheeks. She shook her head slightly.

"I want to hear the words."

She hesitated. Her voice sounded weak and needy. If Aleron were here now, she'd at his feet. "I loved him."

"Yes," Nightshade nodded.

Her body quivered. He wanted to go to her, comfort her, make love to her, drink from her and let her drink from him. But none of it would matter. Even dead, Aleron was a wedge between them, maybe even more so than if he were still alive, or whatever this state he had brought them into could be called. And he not only kept them from one another, he kept them from themselves.

She began to climb down off the stage.

"Stay there!" he shouted.

She looked afraid. Lonely. Now was not the time to comfort her; he had to keep reminding himself of that or he would do something stupid and Aleron would win. "The rest."

She leaned back against the edge of the stage. "I woke in my own bed. It was the next night. My head felt empty and my body hollow. Everything sounded so loud, and I heard so many noises, all mixed together. I saw light through my eyelids. Shadows. I didn't want to move.

"Aleron's voice seemed to be sliding around inside my head. 'Open your eyes, beloved.'

"I must have opened them, because his face was there, the long white hair framing his angelic features, those sparkling grey eyes that talked about other worlds, wonderful places of passion and despair. He looked like a proud father, eyeing his offspring for the first time. Delight. Wonder. Boredom.

"When I saw that, it hurt. I didn't know why he looked bored, and I was afraid to ask, but I felt inadequate in some basic way. Do you know what I'm talking about?"

"Yes." Nightshade remembered the look and knew the feeling of self-doubt intimately.

"He fed me right away and only when my limbs came alive and I began to breathe again did it hit me that I hadn't been feeling anything at all. That night I was completely out of it."

"How did he feed you?"

Suddenly she shoved away from the stage and stormed up the aisle. "You don't have any fucking right to know that!"

He was out of his seat and on her before she could defend herself. "Don't tell me what rights I have! You wouldn't be here if it wasn't for me."

"I owe you for eternity? Just tell me how to pay you back, so we can be on even footing, okay?"

"You can even it by telling me what I need to know. Give me the truth for a change!"

She looked caught for a second. Her arm swung out to slap him, but he snagged her wrist. He grabbed her hair and pulled her head back, exposing her throat. He felt ferocious and made sure to let her see his teeth and his fury.

"You're not my equal yet, honey." He wasn't about to put up with these remnants of mortal embarrassment and guilt. Too much was at stake.

Cheryl backed down, an animal that recognizes the other is dominant; this battle cannot be won. The blaze in her eyes dimmed as her body took on a submissive posture.

He let her go but turned away. If she was going to attack, now was the time. He had turned his back on her to test her. Did she feel any loyalty to him? If she didn't, he'd better know about it before it was too late.

Cheryl didn't attack. Instead she took a seat across the aisle from his. Now that they both sat and faced each other, she stared directly at him. Hatred flared in her eyes from this safer distance. If loyalty existed behind the enmity, he couldn't see it.

"Mostly I took it from his cock. Every night he fed me, he fucked me. Happy? Or do you want the details of that too?"

Those icy words chilled the air between them.

"You enjoyed yourself, I presume."

"Yes. Of course. Didn't you enjoy getting fucked by Aleron?"

Colder. Her attack wasn't going to be physical, but it was as sharp as her claws. "The plot's slowing down, honey. Act Two. Move it along."

"There's nothing more to say. I fed, I fucked. It was fun."

"And when did it stop being fun?"

"It never stopped."

"Then cut to Act Three."

"What do you want to know?"

"The climax."

"I was with him ten days. When we weren't eating or screwing, I was listening. He talked about love. And despair. And alchemy. He was an alchemist, you know."

Nightshade felt his jaw clench which fortunately kept his mouth shut. He knew. All of that. And far more than she did.

"He showed me this chemical experiment. He heated cinnabar in a kind of tall copper pot he called an athanor, until he had quicksilver.

Then he added something—potassium metal, I think he said, but I'm not sure—and it became a solid. And then he put that in water and it began to steam and flames shot up. And the quicksilver fell out. It was magical! He was trying to show me how the universe works. Nothing is ever lost, it just changes form. He said our state is like this too. We aren't dead in the usual sense, what most people think of as death. We're just in a different form. We appear to be solid but it depends what ingredients you add." Nightshade let a sound of disgust erupt. It didn't dampen her soliloquy.

"One night—the only night he took me out of the apartment—he showed me how he could disappear. We went to an old cemetery, the one across town, where that famous poet's buried? It was a beautiful night. The sky clear. A moon so full we had plenty of light to read the inscriptions as we strolled among the crypts and simple graves. Aleron stopped at a gorgeous mausoleum, built of grey marble, with a stone Gabriel sitting on the peaked roof, and the faces of two cherubs on either side of the door.

"'Walk back towards the path, ten paces,' he told me. 'Say my name, then turn around.'

"I did. When I turned, Aleron was gone. I searched the cemetery and called him for half an hour, more frantic every second. Suddenly, I came around to the front of the mausoleum again and there he was, leaning against the doorway between the cherubs, smiling, just like when I last saw him.

"'Where did you go?'

"'It is you who disappeared, beloved. I have been here all along.'

"He swore to me he hadn't moved. And when I stepped back a dozen feet and looked—the way he told me to look, not with my eyes but with my imagination, expecting him not to be there— suddenly I saw how he blended with the shadows, the way his body moulded to the pillars and how the grey marble doorway camouflaged him. His form subtly shifted and fused. The silence made him completely disappear, at least to my eyes. He had become part of the structure and I couldn't see him at all."

"Theatrical tricks."

Her head jerked up, back to the reality of the theater, the reality of him. She shook her head. "No. Not a trick."

He jumped to his feet and paced the aisle with long strides, struggling unsuccessfully to keep his fury in check. "Don't be so naive! Do you think you're the first bitch he charmed with that illusion? Aleron the Great Magician. The Metamorphose! Come and see the creature with the supernatural powers of a deity! Watch him turn his body into blood and the blood into wine for your consumption, just like Christ!"

His voice echoed through the empty theater for a second until her words slashed the air. "You saw that, didn't you? And more. And you're jealous. He's what you're not. Great."

He moved faster than her eye could track. She jumped to her feet and turned, startled, staring up at him behind her. "Yes," he said, "I watched the Great Master of Mirage take his best shots and learned at his hallowed feet. But you were just getting to the good part. How you charred him. Details."

"Why are you being so cruel? You say you once loved him."

"Because this Theater of the Absurd has run long enough and I'm bored. Intermission's over; it's time for the final curtain."

They both sat and glared at one another. Waiting.

She gripped the arm of the seat hard. Her knuckles turned white. Her face had become a plaster mask. A Greek tragedy was underway here and he didn't like the tone. "Don't break the furniture," he said lightly.

She looked down, then up. All he could offer her was a strained smile. It was enough, apparently; her face softened and that perpetual hunger, for him, for blood returned. She wanted him inside her. His cock. The blood cruising his veins. But more, she wanted Aleron, and he knew that. It gave him the hard edge he needed to push her. He had to know it all.

"Get to it if you want any kind of snack before bed."

Hope filled her face. He wasn't delusional enough to believe it all focused on him, but he would take what he could from her. All that Aleron had left.

"He liked to tie me up, with thin copper chains, binding me to the bed, to the doorframe, anywhere, my body naked, pried open. I guess those chains wouldn't hold me now, but then, I was so weak. And hungry. All the time. 'Understand that I possess you,' he said, every night, all night long. It was like chanting, the words eating into my brain until every cell of my body knew it was true. 'I possess you, I possess you.' I did belong to him.

"I watched him like a puppy watches its master, each time he moved, a slight gesture, even when he wasn't moving, just staring out the window as if waiting for something. I was desperate for attention. I existed in a state of perpetual hunger. Throughout the night he fed me drops of blood, randomly, whetting my appetite. It was never enough. I was always hungry, wanting. Sometimes he talked, about the others, about you, and that terrified me. He was beyond misery. He said there was no one left, and no way to get high. He's done it all—many times over. I tried, but my words didn't affect him. Instead, his depression sucked me down with him until at times I thought I'd smother under the despair; my heart turned to lead in my chest and I didn't even have the energy to breathe. And then suddenly he would be playing with my body, bringing me close to orgasm, sucking and biting my nipples until I was screaming for release, licking my clitoris, entering me, anywhere, everywhere. And always he stopped short. My body writhed and throbbed. I've never been so excited. There were moments when I felt: *if he just looks at me I'll come.* But, of course, those were the moments when he wouldn't look my way at all, or he would leave the apartment and I'd be alone with desires that nearly drove me crazy. I spent a lot of time crying. But my tears didn't move him. Neither did my anger. All I know is that the cycle continued. Endlessly. The feeding. The silence. His despair. The wild sex. And throughout it all, the words: 'I possess you,' over and over. I've never felt so completely and deliciously helpless, so overwhelmed with passion. Can you understand that?"

He couldn't answer.

"Aleron became my every thought. Anything he asked, I would have done it for him. I know he knew that. And when he told me to open the curtains and chain him to the bed and sleep in the trunk, I did it, without thinking about what he was asking, never considering the sunlight, trusting him like a child. Hoping he would reward me for being obedient."

Her shoulders fell forward and shook as she sobbed. "I didn't know. I didn't let myself know."

Nightshade moved across the aisle. He crouched down and took her fragile shoulders in his hands. "Stop it, Cheryl! Trust me, he's not worth crying over. Tell me the rest. Quickly."

"Why?" Her face was a mask of agony. An agony he felt too sharply.

Seeing it smeared across her features steeled him.

"You can cry for him for the rest of eternity but right now you'll tell me what I want to know!"

The stern tone sliced into her. He knew it would be hard for her to forgive him for what she perceived as callousness. But he had no choice. They could huddle here together in a pool of self pity and endless longing, or he could do what needed to be done.

She pulled back, shaking free. Her moist eyes hardened into cool emeralds, flashing a barely restrained hatred. "The end? It's simple. I got out of the trunk to find a bed full of ashes in the shape of my lover."

"What else?"

Her lips pressed hard together, as though she might not tell him. Suddenly it was as though she realized this particular scene wasn't worth fighting over. "I found a letter. In his jacket pocket."

"Saying?"

"Saying what I should do. Gather the ashes up in the sheet. Bury them. Come to you."

"Where did you bury them?"

"Why do you want to know?"

"He's dead. Why do you care?"

"Because I loved him. You didn't. That's obvious. Whatever happened between you wasn't love from your end. You just want to get even because he stopped loving you. I can see that now."

"You don't see anything. He's got you mesmerized from the grave. He seduced hundreds over the centuries. You think what you feel is love. It's bondage, and those pretty copper chains you romanticize about were just the most obvious part of the package. It's getting late. And I'm tired of this tragedy. I want to know where you buried the remains of the great metaphysician."

"I'm not going to tell you."

"Don't even think that, because you're going to tell me!"

She shook her head. "You can hurt me, I know you can, but I won't betray Aleron."

Time was running out. It was a big risk but he had to do something. "I'm not going to hurt you, Cheryl, not in the way you think. But I will deprive you of blood. And since you seem to love being chained up, I can do that too, and lick your cunt just the way Aleron did, so you can get off while you're starving."

"Bastard!" She flew at him, her nails sharpened talons, slashing into the flesh of his cheeks, her jaws snapping towards his throat.

They struggled briefly before he brought her down. His weight pressed her face-first to the carpet until she was gnawing at the fibers. He held her wrists behind her neck and his body weight kept her pinned. In time they would be more equal. For the moment he still had the edge. "Spare yourself a few grams of agony. Tell me where I can find the remains of the recently departed."

"No! He's mine! I love him! You never did!"

He let her sob and scream and curse him. But eventually all the crying and bucking against his body as she tried to throw him off stopped. As she lay under him, her breathing returning to normal, he patted her hair, a simple act of comfort; he felt the will seep out of her like a spirit drifting away from the earth.

"What are you going to do?" she asked in a small, frightened voice.

"Finish it."

"What does that mean? I told you he's dead."

"Where did you bury him."

"Why can't you trust me? I've given you everything else, why isn't that enough? Why do you always stay hidden from me?"

"Because you still love him."

"I love you."

"Not the way you love him."

"Aleron's dead. Can't you let him rest in peace?"

"Peace? For who? You? Me? Don't try to make me into him, Cheryl. If you care about us—"

"No, if you care about us. And I wonder just how much you do care."

"Meaning?"

"You'll destroy us. What we have, what we can have together,... Why can't you let it be?"

She pushed back and he let her up. They both sat on the floor crosslegged, facing each other, the tension thick as an invisible wall that threatened to become visible. "I didn't know I could love you," she said softly. "As much as I loved him. But what you're asking is destroying that love. I guess it comes down to a choice: You can have me or you can have Aleron's ashes to desecrate. If you care about me at all, you'll forget about him."

He didn't even pause. "Where are the ashes?"

She looked as if he'd slapped her. Then her face became stony. She got to her feet and glared down at him. "The cemetery. Across town. The mausoleum I told you about."

She hurried down the aisle and up onto the stage. Her boot heels clacked hard against the floorboards as she crossed to the back. Just before she exited, she turned. Light danced off her perfect cheekbones. Those large green eyes had narrowed and turned to hard jade. "I won't be back, you know."

She turned and he heard the stage door slam.

He brought his hands together and clapped them three times slowly, despairingly. "Bravo. Encore." But she didn't return. And he didn't go after her.

Metadrama

———✦———

Under the unearthly glow of a full moon, Cheryl watched Nightshade's shadowy form slip between the gravestones. He treated the three low steps leading to the silent tomb as one but stopped at the grey marble door with Gabriel poised for flight above his head. He seemed to be procrastinating, or maybe steeling himself to enter. His hands reached out crucifixion-style and grasped the two stark cherub faces. Suddenly he snapped his head to the left and stared straight in her direction.

Cheryl ducked back behind the large oak, but not in time. She stepped into the moonlight.

"Coming in for the show, or do you just want to catch the sound effects?"

She hated herself for being here, for spying on Nightshade—especially after what happened at the theater tonight—, for trying to protect Aleron's memory, a memory that, the more she thought about it, the more she realized how tainted it was with something dark and unpleasant she didn't want to look at. But she was here. She might as well see it all.

His eyes, intense from stress, watched her. She noticed his hands balled into fists at his sides. His jaw was tight. When she got close enough, it became obvious he'd fed, and a lot, on the way here. The white moonbeams brought out the contrasts in his flushed skin. His full lips were darker than she'd ever seen them and those sun-gold eyes piercing.

He grabbed the padlock she had affixed to the door—as Aleron's note had instructed—and yanked it from the clasp. He shoved the marble door inward and disappeared into the darkness.

She followed on his heels. The cool interior of the mausoleum, the odor of decay, the utter silence, all brought home what had happened so recently. She felt claustrophobic and wanted to run from this house of the dead. She herself should be dead, or was she dead?—she didn't remember dying. And yet it now seemed as though she would never die. Maybe that very knowledge made this place both attractive and repulsive. And then there were Aleron's remains.

Small slatted windows—air vents really—let in moonlight. The stone coffin took up most of the space. Aleron had anticipated his own death, apparently—the crypt, the coffin. That had unnerved her. When she brought his remains here, the lid, carved with his effigy, was already pushed aside at the top corner. A small triangle lay open, just enough to allow the sheet containing his ashes to be surrendered to their permanent home. It took all her strength to shift that corner of the lid the twelve inches needed to seal up the casket for what she thought at the time was forever. And now she was back, with Nightshade. She didn't know exactly what he had in mind but she knew it would be a violation of some kind, and that she couldn't bear.

"Please," she begged. "Let's go away. Get a fresh start..."

The two copper chains Aleron's letter had instructed her to secure around the coffin were still there. Nightshade snapped both apart. He shoved the lid hard. Stone scraped stone then the lid plunged over the edge of the sarcophagus and crashed to the concrete floor, breaking into half a dozen large chunks. Dust clouded the air. "'Alas, poor Yorick,...' Nobody knew you well, babe."

Cheryl noticed the interior of the coffin was copper-lined, like the copper chains Aleron had bound her with, like the athanor. She fingered the ankh around her neck.

Carefully Nightshade's slender fingers untied the black sheet and spread it open. Even Aleron's bones had burned to dust, making her wonder the night she'd found him if he had been conscious as his body dissolved. To preserve her own sanity, she'd decided he couldn't have been. Now he was a pile of ash, as grey as his eyes had been, but lusterless by comparison.

Her body trembled. She could hardly breathe. Something awful was about to happen. She stepped towards Nightshade. "Please. I'm begging you. Don't..."

His head jerked in her direction. The look on his face silenced her fast. It was as though she'd never seen him before. He was hard, unbending. Obsessed. Her body began to spasm. She had never seen anything like what stood before her now.

He must have caught his reflection in her eyes. "Come here," he said softly, pulling her close. "Trust me!"

She wanted to. She needed to. "But, what?..."

His mouth captured hers, pulling, twisting, sucking on her lips hungrily, prying them apart so that his tongue could enter. She tasted blood and her brain shut down. His hands, frantic, rode her body, and their heat made her as desperate as he was.

She tore at his pants. As her fingers stroked his swollen flesh, he turned her around and bent her forward. The space between the coffin and the wall behind was narrow; he made her lean all the way across the casket. She gripped the far edge of the icy stone.

He picked up one of the copper chains and wrapped it around her waist, twice, then around his own. It was a symbolic gesture; chains wouldn't hold her now, at least she didn't think so. The hand holding the chain gathered her skirt at the slit and pulled the fabric back and up. His other hand slid between her legs and ripped the crotch of her panties away. She gasped and he pulled the chain taut.

She stared at the ashes two feet from her face as Nightshade entered her. He slid in deep and she moaned. Her long hair hung down and brushed Aleron's remains. The burning walls inside her wept as they compressed. Nightshade's thrusts created ripples of charged energy. Small eruptions shot sparks through her body that returned to her vagina in the span of a breath. Within seconds she clutched the edge of the coffin violently. Stone crumbled in her hands. She arched her back and screamed when the inferno exploded.

He was still inside her, still firm. In a second, when she recovered a bit, she would give him pleasure, any way he wanted it. But for another moment, while she found her way back to ground level...

His hands slid down her forearms and locked on. He brought her arms up and crossed them over her chest then pulling her back upright. Her head fell against his shoulder. He lifted her right wrist to his mouth and she sighed, anticipating the dark kiss. Instead, pain seared her.

His long teeth sliced too deep into her wrist, at an angle, tearing things that shouldn't be torn. Quickly he pierced his own wrist. "What are you doing?" she asked, nervous. When he didn't answer, she began to struggle. "Let me go!" But he'd fed so much, and recently, he was far stronger. He bit into the artery of her left wrist, and his own. Then he forced her over the coffin again.

"Stop! Don't take my blood!" she screamed. "I don't have enough!" Blood pumped from the severed arteries and gushed from the veins onto the ashes below. It jerked out of her body. With each crimson jetstream, she weakened. As her energy dimmed, so did her ability to fight him.

Nightshade was a rock. She shrieked and ranted, kicking, twisting, finally crying bloody tears of fear and frustration until she could no longer hold her head up. Within seconds most of the blood had left her, wasted over a pile of moldering ash. The wounds in her wrist lay open but nothing much was coming out. She felt empty, and near collapse.

He held her there until all the blood from his own body had saturated the remains. If he felt as depleted as she, Cheryl had no idea where he found the strength to pull her up and keep both of them vertical.

Her mind flowed down a dark river, melding with the current, diluted by the expanding black liquid to become every sea in the world.

She couldn't see clearly, or hear. And when the wet copper scent tapped her olfactory nerve, at first it was unidentifiable. Her eyelids cracked open to blurry vision. No, it was not her eyesight.

Smoke swelled from the coffin. Cheryl watched transfixed. It was as if the cold blood had splattered onto a hot grill. Sizzling. Acrid vapours billowed into the air, clouding the room, enveloping them in a dense haze.

The air grew glacial, laced with the stench of putrefaction. The building rumbled beneath her feet. Her teeth chattered uncontrollably, her limbs went numb.

A low snarl turned her nerves to ice water. Something dark lifted up through the fog and took on a spectral shape. Two dead grey circles with fiery centers pierced the gloom.

As if a preternatural wind blew through the crypt, the mist cleared.

Three beings inhabited the marble chamber.

Aleron's ashen eyes aligned like magnets, attracted to the iron in the dried blood on her arms, on Nightshade's raw wounds.

His mouth clamped onto Nightshade's wrist, sucking, a white tongue lashing out. When he'd gotten all that was possible, the seated skeleton glared at her. Rice paper flesh stretched over bone, nearly hairless. Scarred. Lips bent on siphoning from her what she no longer had burned like dry ice.

His eyes began to sparkle, tinted window panes when the sun hits. It reminded her of the first time she saw them, when they had been all that existed for her. But his face was a hideous gargoyle alive with madness. She could not stand to look at such distortion, but she could not turn away.

She sobbed from the pain of being bled dry. She tried but couldn't pull away. Aleron didn't seem to notice. Nightshade did. He yanked her backwards, hard. Aleron's mouth came away with a loud popping sound; the suction had been broken.

Those eyes swirled in demented brilliance. She was drawn towards them and what lay beyond. But he was feral, ravenous; he would have gone after her for more if she'd had any more. Before she realized it, his icy hands reached under her t-shirt and caressed her breasts, chilling her, thrilling her. She leaned back against Nightshade. Cold seeped through her pores, tightening her nipples, freezing what little energy she had left, but she couldn't stop him.

Aleron ran a hand over Nightshade's gaunt face, down his chest, down to his crotch, his steely pinprick eyes never leaving the faded suns. "Phenomenal. To die the true death and return. No experience compares. Agony equals transformation. I am truly a god. Your god.

"And you of my creation, you are so vulnerable now. And I am famished. You should have brought more; I told you I would need more."

"You...you knew you were coming back?" Cheryl gasped, astonished.

Nightshade pushed away the hand fondling his cock and zipped his pants. His eyes flickered, as if their light might go out. "You got the starring role in this vehicle," he said to Aleron. "I played my part. What more do you want?"

Cheryl broke away from both of them. She moved to the foot of the coffin; the chain around her waist loosened. "I don't get it."

"Nightshade vowed an oath decades ago. Should he learn of my death, he was compelled to revive me at the next full moon. Following my instructions, of course."

Suddenly it dawned on her. "You died so you could come back. And sent me to Nightshade because you knew he'd bring you back." Confusion gripped her again. "Why would you do that?" But she was afraid she knew the answer.

"And why not?" As he climbed out of the coffin, his eyes left hers and moved to Nightshade's. His rictal grin bared enormous eye teeth, stained scarlet. "My theory proved correct."

"Then this production has finished its run," Nightshade said.

"Has it?"

Cheryl held onto the coffin with both hands. She had to. "You used me," she said in a small voice. "Both of you."

Aleron stroked her cheek absently. He looked to Nightshade and shook his head in confusion, as though he had no idea what she was talking about. Nightshade only stared at him.

But it was clear to her now. Aleron had put her through agony, just so he could get off big time. And Nightshade had helped him. At her expense.

Nightshade let the cool wall prop him up. He studied the slim naked form, severely scarred from the flames that had devoured him. Those scars would fade, in time. That was too bad. Aleron wouldn't have anything physical to remind him, and his memory had become a labyrinth of crumbling medieval script fragments, the lines of which he had a habit of misquoting.

Nightshade had his own scars, emotional in nature. But now they seemed to be nothing more than a mid-summer night's dream. Yet he had always remembered his dreams vividly, and his nightmares.

His term of indenture was over. For the first time in his immortal existence he was a free agent. Aleron had bled to create him. He had given his blood to recreate Aleron. Nightshade felt the moment the bond snapped. Now the set was clear and only the actors were left. Predictably, Aleron didn't seem to notice the change, or at least he didn't let on.

"The pain of death is nothing to the pain of rebirth," Aleron said, pontificating as usual. "Dissolution is harsh but predictable and follows a course in keeping with what we already understand. But to be reformed...I did not know what I would become but knew I would be-come greater than I had been. Never less. Of course, I could not be less than I am."

Aleron was a user, incapable of love. Did he feel any emotions or had they all shrivelled centuries ago? Too many nights Nightshade had lain in the darkness terrified he might one day become Aleron: jaded, hopeless. Desperate for something or someone to fill his existence with meaning, if only for moments here and there.

"I glimpsed neither Jehovah nor Satan. I hovered in a chrysalis between life and death simply waiting for a sign of the alteration to occur. It is a state much like sleep but with more conscious awareness. Those such as yourselves would not easily tolerate this state. I, however, am more than sentient and my will made the difference."

More insults. Low shots. Subtle, like a chilly gust. Aleron had to be on top. Always. Knocking him off that self- perpetuating pedestal would be sheer pleasure.

Cheryl stood motionless, looking confused. Angry. Not quite able to believe what was happening. Aleron flirted with her, curling her hair around his fingers, tongue-kissing her palm, easing in close, as if she should forget that he had used her. A seductive smile played across his lips. He was so handsome. Irresistible. Despite how distorted his body was now, those classical features, framed only by wisps of white hair, were remarkable. His grey eyes arrested both mortals and immortals alike. Nightshade remembered staring at that face and that body for what had seemed like an eternity and never tiring of the sight. Aleron's looks were his blessing and his curse. He'd never had to work at immortality. There had been few challenges. Now there were none.

Aleron fingered the ankh lying in the hollow of her throat. "Copper, a feminine metal, the symbol of Venus and Frida, the conductor of life and death. You understand, only through your being may we gods move with ease. I am truly immortal now. Nightshade is in error, as I told him many times. And I have proven this, to you both. I sailed the river Styx and have returned to confirm what I knew before I first embarked on this alchemical journey: there is no purpose to existence."

Like a character too ignorant to realize he's destined to be written out of a script, Aleron kept up the charming discourse. But he was not talking with them, or even to them. He'd never been inclusive, except to further his purposes. And yet, some part of him must know that the theater was closing and the company disbanding.

He glided around the crowded space gracefully, theatrically, his style unique, admirable. He stared at Cheryl but spoke to Nightshade. "Such submissiveness. A perfect container. A true enchantress. We three belong together, you know. Will you look after her for me? Until I return?"

Abdicating his responsibility. As always. He didn't want either of them but it was not his way to say so. And he wouldn't admit even to himself that they were no longer his possessions.

Nightshade wanted to hate Aleron, but hate was no longer an option. He pitied this one who had survived centuries, enduring an anguish so great he couldn't even admit it to himself. Aleron had never been able to handle truth. And the truth had become monstrous: he had reached the end of his time. There were no more plots to twist. No new plays would be written in limbo.

Cheryl was about to confront him. Nightshade moved up behind her. His fingers on the back of her neck sent a message, as if his thought planted itself in her head. Her mouth closed.

"I'll take care of her."

"Good." Aleron glanced outside. He role was not an enviable one: warrior crazed from too many battles. He didn't know he'd lost the war. He paraded the battlefield like a hero, when in fact he was a figure of scorn.

He leaned in. His lips brushed Cheryl's, then Nightshades. Behind the windows of his eyes a shadowy being fled the stage. They would not meet again.

Before Aleron could sense that, he moved out into the ivory light painting the sky. He did not turn when he asked in a quiet voice, "What it is you used to love to quote at me? Concerning reliance."

"'I have always relied on the kindness of strangers.'"

Aleron paused only a heartbeat, then moved briskly down the steps and across the graveyard. The air thinned; he was gone.

"Why did you do it?" Cheryl demanded. Her eyes flashed fury. "You could have brought him back yourself. Why drag me into this?"

He stepped towards her. "Isn't it obvious?" He took the copper ankh in his hand and ripped the chain from her throat. He threw Aleron's 'gift' outside.

The impact of that action hit home but she couldn't restrain herself. "But he fucked both of us over and you let him get away with it!"

Aleron had wounded her. Nightshade hoped he could repair the damage.

"You had the chance," she went on. "Why didn't you tell him...?"

His finger touched her lips. "'Swift as a shadow, short as any dream, Brief as the lightning in the collied night, That, in a spleen, unfolds both heaven and earth, And ere a man hath power to say, 'Behold!' The jaws of darkness do devour it up: So quick bright things come to confusion.'"

Her eyes flickered, then softened as understanding seeped in. "You could have crushed him, but you didn't." She exhaled, as if she'd been holding her breath for a long time. "I guess it's you who loved him most."

Suddenly pain flashed across her pale face. "I'm so hungry."

"I know. So am I. But the sun will be up any minute. There's no time to get back to the theater. We should stay here. Barricade the door, use the coffin to block the light. We'll be safe. If you want to stay with me, that is."

She hesitated. Her green eyes were clear, but did she know she had a choice? Him. Aleron. Neither of them. It was the last he worried most about.

"Do you want me to stay?" she asked.

"'Doubt thou the stars are fire; Doubt that the sun doth move; Doubt truth to be a liar; But never doubt I love.'"

Her arms circled his neck. He pulled her close and kissed her lips longingly, lovingly. She was a feather in his arms but her essence filled his heart.

They blocked the door from the inside and nestled in safety until daylight once more gave way to the world of darkness.

Erotic
Bloodsuckers

Dark Seduction

———◦◦◦———

"He's the one I told you about," Paula whispered discreetly. Karen allowed her giggling friend to lead her through the maze of cigarette-smoking cocktail-sipping party guests.

"He'd better be worth it," Karen whispered back. "I don't like wasting time or energy."

"He's exactly what you're looking for. And I know he'll find you charming. Would I steer you wrong?" Paula's blue eyes twinkled mischievously, just the way Karen remembered them when the two had met years ago in a high school pottery class. Back then they had become close, very close. Jokingly they used to refer to each other as Bizarre Babe. And now Paula was married, living in a rented chateau outside Paris; Karen wondered just what kind of good luck charm her friend owned that had made all her dreams come true.

Karen and Armand sized each other up. He was a few inches taller, maybe five eleven, and looked a bit older, about thirty. Broad shoulders, medium build, trim, toned. He wore a designer suit, Cardin, she thought, because of the shoulders, double breasted, the color of slate, which accented his dark features. His hair and brows were black but his skin was paler than the perpetual tan most dark-haired men seemed to cultivate. *Looks healthy enough*, she thought. His well-defined, full lips—perfectly shaped, and a pale red—turned up slightly at the corners, without giving the impression he was smiling. His eyes were incredible. Grey or black, she couldn't tell in the subdued light. They stared intensely into hers. *Almost boring into me*, came to mind, and Karen laughed to herself at the Victorianism.

She extended a hand. "Nice to meet you."

Instead of shaking hers, he brought it to his lips, bowed slightly, then kissed the inside of her palm. She could feel the tip of his tongue and shivered. His eyes never left hers.

"Enchante." He spoke very good English, with just the trace of an accent lacing a richly masculine voice. "The pleasure is all mine, or will be," he added, smiling a little. "I'd better warn you—I become obsessed with green-eyed redheads."

She couldn't tell if he was being facetious but decided to play it simple. She laughed, fiddling with her necklace coyly. "How very French." His smile turned fixed.

"Karen's here doing research," Paula said. "For her PhD."

"It's on the supernatural," Karen added.

"A subject close to all our hearts," Armand said.

"It is to mine." There was more of an edge to her voice than she'd intended. He was still holding her hand and she pulled it away.

"I'm not always sarcastic." His voice warmed a little, his eyes became playful. "But I am a cynic. It's the nature of the beast."

Suddenly, two girls, and Karen could only call them that, flounced up to Armand, one on each side. The dark-haired, blue- eyed thing on his left wore a see-through white dress buttoned almost to her chin. Without the barrier of a bra, her firm nipples stretched the fabric to its limit. She grabbed his arm and cooed into his face. The other one, blonde and brown-eyed, dressed in a black leather bustier and spandex bicycle pants wore a studded collar wide enough to conceal her entire throat. Her full lips formed into an exaggerated pout, which made Karen laugh out loud. The girl said something to him in French that Karen suspected meant 'Oh, you're so mean, not paying enough attention to me!'

Karen laughed and Armand scowled. The scene struck her as so ludicrous she had to turn away or she would have laughed in his face.

"Nice to have met you, Mr. Gautier," she mumbled, stumbling off, a hand clamped over her mouth, dragging Paula with her. To her friend, Karen whispered, "And your daughters too."

"Shush!" Paula warned. "He'll hear you."

"We're too far away."

"He has unnaturally acute hearing. I wouldn't get him angry if I were you."

Karen turned to her, surprised. She'd always seen Paula as bold and daring, almost as much as herself. Her friend looked worried and Karen started to ask, "What do you mean?" but they'd arrived at a small group of men, each wearing almost identical three-piece blue suits, France's equivalent of the university professor look. Karen was introduced around before Gary called Paula away.

She got some interested but uninteresting looks, and the four men continued an intellectual discussion, unfortunately, for her benefit, in English. This led to a long discourse by one on the superiority of human intelligence over animal instincts. Karen put in her two cents worth now and then, but generally it was an academic and pedantic discussion, the type she was painfully familiar with, so she just sipped her wine and let her mind wander.

It must have wandered a bit too far because she dropped her clutch purse and one of the men stooped to pick it up. Behind him, looking somewhat amused, Armand Gautier leaned against a pillar. Arms folded easily across his chest. Legs crossed at the ankles. She found herself focusing on the bulge at his crotch. He seemed a fascinating antidote for the babbling tutorials surrounding her.

The one who had retrieved her bag stood and handed it over. She thanked him and tried to look around him surreptitiously. Armand had vanished.

"And your conclusion, Mademoiselle?"

Karen had no idea what she was being asked about but said, "I'd rather not comment just yet, until I've heard more," which seemed to satisfy the asker.

"Here's Armand. He'll have an opinion," someone said.

Gautier approached. He didn't look at her. "An opinion on what, Etienne?"

"On the superiority of the mind."

"No. Passion!" another argued.

Karen said nothing.

Armand glanced at each of the men. He was suave, sophisticated, a polished jewel among chunks of rough rock.

"Perhaps an analogy will clarify my views," he said.

Smooth as bushed silk, she thought.

"For the sake of argument, let's assume we're all animals—horses, or even dogs, if you like. Here we are, a pack of five studs. And one bitch." Armand glanced at Karen, a taunting smile on his lips. One of the others laughed nervously.

"We five would be completely driven by our instincts. Given the chance, we would fight, jockeying for power, biting, wounding, until one dominated all the others. Again, for convenience, we'll say I'm the winner."

The entire room seemed to have become silent and Karen noticed that a small crowd had gathered, attracted by the feeling of electricity in the air. Paula stood anxiously to one side. When she caught Karen's eye, she gestured for her to come away. But Karen was curious.

"And then the reward. The pursuit of the female," Armand continued, looking directly at Karen.

She knew her face flamed, but she was intrigued. At last this dull party was picking up.

"I would hunt you down, Mademoiselle Linden, tirelessly, throughout the night, allowing you no rest, insinuating myself, nudging, prodding, insisting, wearing you down, second by second, until at last, in a moment of weakness, exhaustion even, you submit to me. Then I would mount you—a bitch in heat—sinking my teeth into your neck, drawing blood, keeping you still while I breach you unmercifully until I'm completely satisfied. And then? Then I'd move on to the next challenge."

The room was a tomb. Even the Baroque trio had stopped playing. Armand stared at her, holding her with his dark eyes. She knew she should have been insulted and angry. *Maybe it's the wine*, she thought. She burst into laughter, easing everyone's tension.

"Mr. Gautier, you've got a colorful imagination. You must have a pretty active fantasy life." Karen downed the rest of her wine, placed the empty glass on the table, then turned to walk away. She could feel the heat from his eyes burning against her. For a moment, she toyed with the glazed porcelain beads that circled her throat. Suddenly, she spun around and glared at Armand. His eyes were mocking, his face condescending. "With such a chauvinistic attitude, I'll bet fantasy is about your limit."

She knew it was a crude remark, but it was enough to get her across the room so she could exit dramatically onto the glassed-in balcony. Behind, she heard a sardonic laugh followed by people stirring. Then, music.

Outside, she scanned the grounds of the chateau, absorbed by the enchanting nightscene, trying to forget about the silly encounter.

The estate Paula and Gary had rented for the second year of their appointment with the *Comité Illusionniste d'Expertise des Phénomènes Paranormaux* was large. Manicured lawns glowed an eerie green under the artificial lights. Dense clusters of dark twisted trees created a small magical wood. She could see a river, the water flickering behind the October foliage. The scent of horses and forest creatures saturated the air with a rich sensual earthiness. Nearby, a clock began striking out midnight, the witching hour.

Karen heard a noise behind her and turned to see Armand on the balcony. He closed and locked the doors. She was safe—help just a scream away—still, she felt vulnerable.

He moved toward her. "You have an acid tongue, Mademoiselle, as caustic as my own. That's rare in a woman."

"And you, Mr. Gautier, have a foul mouth."

He crossed his arms over his chest. "I meant it when I said I find you attractive. Now you're even more alluring, bewitching almost. I'm going to enjoy making love to you."

"Well, you'll have to use your active imagination because that's the only way it'll happen," she said, trying to brush past him.

He caught her arm.

"Let me go or I'll scream."

"If you like sound-effects, go ahead. No one's coming to your rescue."

"More cynicism?" She felt nervous.

"Not at all. Simply an observation of human nature. Of course they'd like to help, but none are brave enough to take me on. I have a reputation."

"I can imagine. Look, I'm not interested in indulging any of your little fetishes, whatever they are."

"Aren't you."

He grabbed her face and kissed her mouth wildly, filling her with his tongue. Karen tried to knee him in the groin and clobber him with her purse, but he was exceptionally strong. In seconds he had her arms pinned behind her. He backed her up against the glass wall.

This is ridiculous, she told herself. *I'm at a party, in a foreign country, held captive on a balcony by a demented fiend.* She felt embarrassed, angry, and oddly excited. *This can't be happening,* she assured herself.

He held her wrists with one hand and used his other to undo the top of her dress so he could touch her breasts. He was pressed up against her, so she knew he was erect. He lifted her skirt and his fingers slid under her pantyhose and inside her. She was wet, and now they both knew it.

He looked her in the eye, laughing. "Why don't you just spread your legs, Mademoiselle Linden? I'd be more than happy to breach you."

"If you think you're going to rape me, you'll have to do it without my help and, believe me, you'll have a hell of a time."

He laughed again, this time throwing his head back. She noticed his teeth and couldn't quite believe what she was seeing; the two incisors were far longer and more pointed than the rest.

Karen struggled hard, sweating, but couldn't get out of his grip. Her sprayed-into-place hair style had collapsed and her long hair hung in her face so that she couldn't even see. She knew she must look wild. Armand brushed the fiery strands back from her damp forehead. His eyes were bright and large, almost feral. The scent of a musky after-shave and something even more earthy, came off his body. He didn't look quite so cynical now.

Karen knew she should be furious, and even tried to work herself up to it, but the whole thing was such a shock, so spontaneous, and, she hated to admit it, she felt excited.

He kissed her again, a slow passionate kiss, their mouths opening, tongues connecting. When they broke apart his voice was low as he whispered in her ear, "You are a bitch in heat, aren't you? Or is it witch?"

All at once it dawned on her how much control he had and how out of control she was. Too, she felt embarrassed. He'd caught a glimpse of her true nature. "And you're a monster!" she said angrily.

But he only laughed. He let her go, walked to the doors, unlocked them and rejoined the party.

Karen was mortified. She quickly fixed herself up before anyone had a chance to see her disheveled state. As she picked a dark hair off the front of her dress, she asked herself, *what's the matter with you, letting him get so far? And worse, you even liked it!*

She stormed inside, found Paula and frantically related recent events.

"Here," her friend said, handing Karen a fresh glass of wine. "Forget it."

"You're joking! I just told you he tried to rape me."

"Well, at least you got him interested." Paula's turquoise eyes twinkled.

"Oh Mistress of Understatement!" Karen snapped.

"I warned you he's strange. You're the one who insisted on an introduction. Armand's well-known here, and powerful. Nobody goes against him. Consider yourself lucky nothing worse happened."

"Paula, I can't believe I'm hearing this from you."

"Believe it. This isn't like our old school tricks. If you want my advice, you'll forget the whole thing," she said with a look on her face Karen had never seen.

Karen glanced around the room helplessly. Armand stood beneath the chandelier surrounded by his two girls and a couple of younger men, the center of attention. He made a remark and one of the girls turned in Karen's direction, laughing.

"Maybe everybody else is afraid," Karen said, more to herself than to Paula, "but my name's not going to be added to what's probably a long list of his victims!"

Before Paula could intervene, Karen strode over to him.

Armand stopped talking.

"Mr. Gautier, not only are you a chauvinist, but you're an incredibly pompous bore, and a brute. Rotting in Hell would be too good for you!" She tossed the contents of her glass in his face.

He turned so that the full force of it missed him. Still, his shirt and jacket were soaked. Before anything more could happen, Karen made her way to the door.

"I need a taxi," she told the butler.

"Pardon, Mademoiselle, but there are none," he said, looking frightened.

Instead of arguing, she found her coat and left. *I'll walk back to Paris if I have to*, she thought.

She headed down the driveway to the two-lane highway. It was late and dark and there were no cars. *I'll catch a cab if a free one comes by but I'm not going to hitch a ride*, she assured herself.

The stretch of black top only had lights every quarter mile. She stomped along in the darkness until she came to a dim arc of illumination cast by the bright pink lights, then went through it into darkness again. Angry, Karen stumbled on the pebbles of the soft shoulder, finally getting enough of a grip to realize she would manage better on the smooth highway.

This is crazy, she told herself. *You should go back and see if someone will give you a lift. This'll take you all night.* Her heels were ready to crack and her feet were killing her.

A car came up from behind and, despite her determination not to, Karen waved frantically. It swooshed on by.

She trudged on and must have been walking for a good half hour when another car drove up. This one slowed. She put on a smile and waved. The driver of the silver Renault pulled beside her, leaned over and rolled down the window. It was Armand Gautier. "Get in!"

"Never!"

She kept walking and he drove slowly, so he could talk to her. "Don't be stupid. Paris is many kilometers away. I'll drive you there."

Karen stopped to face him, incredulous. "You're really something! First you try to rape me and now you think I'm dumb enough to get into a car with you? You must be insane!" She started walking again.

"Rape?" he called out at her. "That was far from rape. And why do I have the impression you were participating? Even enjoying yourself. Correct me if I'm wrong."

Karen said nothing. She clutched her coat collar in justifiable disdain.

"Mademoiselle Linden. Karen. Get in. I'm not the Devil. I'll simply drive you into Paris and we'll call it a truce."

She didn't bother to answer.

Finally, he said, "One last chance. There are wolves in this area. It's been a hard winter and they're hungry. A boy was killed last week near here, his throat torn open."

This information disturbed her but she pretended it didn't. *Besides*, she thought, *it's probably a lie.* "You're the only wolf on this road!"

Armand drove off in a blast of exhaust. Karen stood quietly, fiddling with her beads, watching the red tail-lights disappear over a rise.

The night was chilly and she folded her arms across her chest to block the cold. She started walking quickly, hoping to warm up. Above, the sky was dotted with stars, and a full moon. Ahead, the air looked hazy, lighter, indicating the city was there, somewhere. She remembered from the drive out fields on both sides of the highway, but in the darkness she couldn't see them.

Off to the right she noticed two small red lights flicker, then they were gone. She saw them again. They moved up and down, back and forth. She noticed other flickering lights but kept walking, vaguely apprehensive, wondering what they were.

When Karen heard the patter of feet behind, she knew. She was in a dark patch, between highway lights. A large wolf trotted at a fast pace through the last glow of pinkness she had passed through. She quickened her own steps. Panicked, she didn't know what to do; she prayed a car would come by.

As she approached the next light, she could see and hear more of them. A quick glance showed her at least three sets of eyes, all gaining. A little ahead, lying on the shoulder, she spotted a gnarled branch. It probably wouldn't help much but it gave her a small feeling of security so she snatched it up.

She ran. The feet behind kept pace. She took off her shoes, thinking she could move faster plus use them as weapons. As she approached the next light, she was panting, her heart pounding double time. She decided to stop there and take up a defensive position; she couldn't go on much farther and at least she'd be able to see them.

Karen turned so she could watch the wolves. One out in front, no more than eight feet away, three others behind. Clammy sweat slid down the small of her back. *They mean to make a meal out of me, that's for sure*, she thought, trembling.

Slowly, she backed up under the glow of the highway lamp, breathing heavily, raising the branch, ready to ward off the attack she knew was coming. The wolf closest to her was big but thin. Starved. He growled, exposing a full set of sharp teeth, letting her know it was only a matter of seconds before he pounced. She eased back a few more steps and hit something solid. Startled, she screamed, but a hand clamped over her mouth, cutting the sound.

"Quiet!"

It was Armand Gautier.

He slid an arm around her waist and pulled her against him. They both faced the wolves. "Don't move or make a sound," he said softly. "Lower the branch slowly and drop it on the ground."

"That's crazy. It's the only weapon we have and–"

"Do it!"

Something made her obey. The sound of wood hitting asphalt seemed deafening.

The wolf closest to them snarled. The ones behind him moved to take up strategic positions. Armand held her close in a proprietary way. He stared intently at the first wolf.

"They have us surrounded," Karen whispered.

"Don't speak!"

Minutes seemed to pass. Finally, he said in a low, hypnotic tone, "The strong must be seduced into submitting to a greater power."

Karen looked at Armand's eyes. The dark, fearless orbs seemed to radiate a red energy. She glanced at the lead wolf. He was staring into those eyes, mesmerized.

The wolf broke the contact. He shook his head a little, turned slowly and trotted off. The rest of the pack followed, heading for the darkness of the fields. The sound of their paws on gravel dimmed to silence.

Armand turned his head. Under the pink light, his eyes seemed to vibrate. His face radiated power and Karen understood that whatever he wanted, he got; no one would stand in his way. *That's what Paula's been trying to tell me*, she realized.

She felt intimidated and pulled back, but he held her tight. "Want that ride now?"

"I guess I don't have a choice," she said, nervously pulling on her dark beads.

"Of course you have a choice! One wolf or four." Laughing, he led her to the car, his arm still capturing her waist.

On the twenty minute drive into Paris, neither spoke. As they pulled in front of Karen's hotel, she unbuckled the seat belt and reached for the door handle. "Thanks for the lift–"

He caught her arm. "I'll take you to dinner tomorrow night. Eight o'clock."

"No, that's okay."

"I insist. You're angry with me. I want to make amends."

"Saving my life is enough. We're even. Let's just forget it, okay?"

"Wear black. The restaurant is small and elegant. Besides, I think black will suit you."

He let her go and she got out. Just before closing the door she said, "Mr. Gautier, we won't be seeing each other again."

"You're weird," she told Armand the next evening at *La Petit Oiseau de Nuit*.

"As are you," he said, first scanning her, and then the oversized menu.

All night and all day, Karen had been occupied by an inner debate. But despite solid arguments against it, something made her put on her black Calvin Klein dress, black beaded necklace and black ankle boots and meet him at the door at eight. He had come in carrying a dozen long-stemmed roses, complete with thorns, such a dark purple they were almost black, and telling her she was beautiful.

Armand ordered in French and they sat silently in the elegant sable booth until the waiter brought wine, white for her, red for him. Armand tilted his glass slowly, letting the contents roll easily along the sides. The entire time his eyes were glued to hers.

"You're tough," he finally said, putting the glass down without taking a sip of the wine. "Opinionated. Lively. Daring. You've got me charmed. Most women are timid."

"I'm flattered, but that's quite a generalization."

"I'm only talking about the women in my experience, and I've had an enormous amount of experience. More than you can imagine."

Karen grinned. She felt reckless, almost diabolical. "Young women don't usually know themselves as well as older women. They don't make many demands, like fidelity, for example." She sipped her wine. Of course, being twenty-seven didn't exactly make her an old hag. But she was comparing herself to the two girls she'd seen him with at the party who looked like they'd barely made it into puberty.

Oddly enough, he seemed undaunted by her confrontation. "You see me as a predator, don't you? A man who likes young girls because they're easy to control. Who flatters himself, probably unduly. Afraid of the challenge of a real woman."

Karen sipped wine, absently playing with the beads around her neck. "That about sums it up."

They were seated next to each other. He moved close, took the glass from her hand and placed in on the table. Gently he cupped her chin, turning her lips to his. His kiss pressed her against the back of the booth. His arm went around her shoulders, his free hand moved down inside her low-cut dress. However secluded their table was by large ferns and ornate partitions, they were in a public place. Karen tried to stop him.

The waiter appeared, serving the food, glancing at them knowingly. Karen, embarrassed, struggled to push Armand off but couldn't budge him. He slipped his hand under her bra and went right to her nipple.

The waiter seemed to take forever but finally departed.

Armand had her almost reclining. His lips had not left hers. His finger tips brought her flesh up firm, forcing her to take in sharp breaths through her nose. She felt light-headed.

Finally, Karen managed to free her mouth from his. "Stop it! What do you think you're doing? And we're in a restaurant, for heaven's sake!"

Laughing, he released her. She noticed his teeth again and shivered. "Heaven is not where I'm from, still, I can take you there. But for the moment, you're in Paris, the City of Enchantment. And passion. Relax." He kissed her lips gently.

The waiter had served rack of lamb in a Dijon sauce and small portions of potatoes, green beans and carrots firmly cooked, but only one plate.

"Aren't you eating?" she asked.

"I will. Later. Go ahead."

The meal was delicious. She dug in and finished quickly, Armand watching her the entire time. She skipped dessert but had more wine. He still hadn't touched his.

"Paula tells me you're an expert on the occult." His eyes were bright and Karen thought he might be amused by the idea.

"I guess you'd say that. Don't laugh, but I'm doing my thesis on vampires."

"Don't worry, I won't laugh."

"There's a man, he was both a Protestant minister and then a Catholic priest, his name was Montague Summers, but you've probably never heard of him. Anyway, he was fixated on vampires and back in the twenties wrote a couple of books. You wouldn't recognize the titles."

"You never know." He picked up the wine glass and rolled the contents around again.

"Well, my thesis challenges Summers' research. I'm out to prove there's no such thing as a vampire. It's all fantasy."

"That shouldn't be difficult. Most people don't believe in vampires."

"More believe than you'd think. But these books by Summers are scholarly works so they're up for attack."

"Why are you so interested in vampires?" He put the glass down. Now he seemed to be taking her seriously.

"I'm not sure." She sat back against the seat. The wine was getting to her. He was looking better and better, his eyes like polished hematite, his body virile, and entirely masculine.

"It's more than a hobby with me," she said, trying to focus on her answer and not his eyes. "I've always been fascinated by the occult, as far back as I can remember. Since I was a kid I've been collecting vampirabilia. And I love watching Christopher Lee videos—he's so seductive, powerful, sexy. I pretend he's seducing me. I'll tell you a secret: whenever I'm watching a vampire film, I want to be a vampire myself. The Bride of Dracula, no less. Submitting to that ultimate power. I guess I've always been hooked."

"But you don't believe vampires exist."

"Nope."

"How can you be sure?"

"Because I've never been able to conjure one up. Look, don't you think if anybody was going to meet a vampire it would be me? Because I'm so interested."

"There's a certain logic to that," he said. He tilted his head, studying her, clearly captivated.

The lines of his face were clean, his skin impossibly smooth. She felt almost compelled to move closer, to touch him.

"What if I told you I was a vampire? What would you think?"

She laughed and coyly fingered her dark, shiny necklace. "I'd think you were trying to make yourself mysterious, so I'd let you have your way with me."

"Do I have to try? To get you to let me have my way?"

Back at the hotel, Armand took Karen to her room.

"I don't want you to come in," she told him, blocking the doorway.

He gave her a sly smile, propping himself against the frame, leaning into her and the room.

"Really!" She backed in and started to close the door, but he came in too.

"Look," she said, but he had her up against a wall, running his hands over her, in one motion lifting her tight skirt to her waist and pulling down both her pantyhose and underwear.

She hadn't been able to turn on the lights but the door was still open, letting in light from the hallway. *I've probably had too much wine,* Karen thought. *His eyes look positively on fire.* While he kissed her lips, he unzipped her dress and slid it down, moving his mouth to one of her nipples. Karen arched her back and groaned. Little waves of electric pleasure rippled through her and her knees felt weak. She didn't know if she could stand up much longer.

He must have closed the door and manoeuvred her to the bed because the next thing she was aware of was that she was wearing only her beads and he only his watch. And he was lying on top of her. Enchanting dream-like Montparnesse street sounds and smells drifted in the open window, filling the room. The full moon encased them in a pale, unearthly brilliance.

His lips pressed onto hers, insistent, and she wanted to open to him. She felt his body; the muscles in his chest, arms and back were tight, sinewy, like a wild animal ready for action. She reached under and held him, which only made him kiss her harder. Then he turned both of them around and licked her wetness. He grew firmer as she tickled him with her tongue and teased him in other ways.

Both were close to release when he turned again and entered her. He was above, his arms supporting him. She stared at his face. So pale, so intense. Almost otherworldly. Her fingers stroked his cheeks and ran through his hair. He felt waxy, unreal.

His thrusts were steady and Karen quivered with desire. She wrapped her legs around his waist forcing him deeper, wanting to possess him and be possessed by him. Little breathy moans escaped her lips.

He lowered himself onto her. He was solid, heavier than she had thought he would be but she liked his weight pressing her. He kissed her again, the most passionate kiss she could remember, his mouth moving, twisting, firmly capturing hers. He moved faster. His lips left hers and found her throat, locking onto it in an even more passionate kiss.

Karen pulled him in, wanting him in a way that was new and startling to her, in a way she couldn't understand and refused to analyze. She invited him to move her, control her and lift her higher and higher. She felt almost delirious with ecstasy. And when she cried out his name, he seemed to break down the walls and reach into the deepest most hidden part of her, filling her, fulfilling her.

"Now what?" she asked. They lay side by side on the bed facing each other. It had been a magical night for Karen. But with the sun an hour away from rising, she could sense that everything between them was rapidly coming to a conclusion.

"Stay here. In Paris." He ran his hand up her thigh, over her hip and back again.

"Just like that? I can't afford this hotel."

"Move in with me. Pack your bags. We'll go to my place right now."

"Do you sleep in a coffin?"

"Why do you ask that?" He sat abruptly, looking at her sharply, his eyes smoky.

"Vampires sleep in coffins, at least if they follow tradition."

He stared at her like someone waking from a trance. "You knew all along."

"Paula told me. You're right. You've got a reputation. But I would have guessed anyway."

"And you're not afraid of me?"

"Why should I be? You're going to offer me immortality, aren't you?"

He hesitated. "I hadn't thought about it."

"Why not? Aren't you lonely and alienated?"

"Not particularly." He got up and put on his shirt, buttoning it from the middle down.

"But you need a companion, right? Everybody does, even vampires. We're more than attracted to each other. And you've already bitten me." She felt the wounds on her neck partially hidden by the beads. "If I drink your blood, that`s it."

He paused, button mid-way through a buttonhole, and shook his head like an animal, trying to clear it. "I feel as if you've had me under a spell or something. I've been used."

"Used? You? Come on! I'm the victim here."

"Wait a minute." He looked upset. "This is bizarre. You planned all this, didn't you?"

"Of course. And now I've got you cornered with the proverbial cross, stake in hand. I've sent a letter to my prof. If he doesn't hear from me, it'll be opened by the police. It names you, describes you. I'm good with clay so I even made a little doll that looks just like you, hair and everything. At least Paula thinks it looks like you. Anyway, I'm sure you can figure out the rest."

Karen smiled. "But don't worry, it won't come to that. So, now we go to your place, I become a vampire, complete my thesis and we spend the rest of eternity together."

He seemed confused, pacing the room. Pink-tinged sweat appeared across his forehead. He held his head as if trying to keep his brain from exploding, trying to sort something out. "But if you knew I was a vampire you must believe vampires exist. So, why the thesis?"

"Because then nobody will ever suspect that I'm one, since it will be on public record that I don't believe."

"This is absurd. You're much stranger than I thought." Suddenly he stopped pacing. A proud and angry look settled on his face. "I won't let you blackmail me. I won't transform you."

"Yes, you will. You have to. Besides, it's too late. I've already bitten you."

"What?" He looked shocked.

"There. On your penis. During the oral part."

Armand's face turned paler than usual. He held onto the head-board for support. "I must have died and gone to Hell. And you're Satan in a siren's body!"

Karen's laugh was almost a cackle. She got onto her knees and hobbled across the mattress toward him, taking his free hand in hers. "Come on, it won't be so bad. We'll have a good time. You can teach me everything you know about being undead and I'll teach you all about the occult. We'll have lots of hot sex, and we'll be together for eternity."

He looked at her with a touch of hysteria clouding his slate eyes. "Eternity's a long time to be with just one woman."

Karen pressed her hot body seductively against his cool one. "But,

Armand, I'm no ordinary woman. Surely you realize that by now."

The seven black clay beads circling her delicate throat rested pre-ternaturally against his chest. It had taken Karen a long time and much patience to work each piece of clay into the shape of a miniature bat, dark wings spread wide, enticing, inviting, each charming in its own way.

The Game

—◦—

"Plebian idiots!" Lawrence muttered. The waiter glanced at him, plunked down the two main courses and hurried away.

"Who?" Fab asked, diving into the rigatoni in tomato sauce.

"The great, barely-washed, vulgar masses, who else?"

"Well, I don't see the problem. It's just a replica."

Fab nodded at the gargoyle above the bar at *Piccolo el Diavolo* that they had been discussing. The image was not a classical one, but a modern interpretation that annoyed Lawrence. It entirely missed the point and instead of capturing evil, it became a nauseating blend of evil and good. A politically-correct gargoyle!

He held up his wine glass. "No one understands the past. They think all of it led to them being born!"

Fab, speaking around a mouthful of pasta, said, "Hey, it's just nostalgia. So they got it a little wrong. This is great food!"

"Nostalgia! Don't talk to me about bloody nostalgia!"

While Fab ate, Lawrence lifted his goblet and stared through the glass-imitating-crystal. Always, that everyman grin slashed across Fab's generous lips, so different from Lawrence's thin, down-turned mouth. Those darker than dark eyes, eyes that struggled and failed to reveal only what Fab wanted them to reveal. Lawrence had trained his own pale orbs until they were masters at exposing nothing. Fab was a natural Game player, both more open and less open than almost any other 'mortal' Lawrence had encountered, as Lawrence liked to think of his prey. He thought of them as mortals because they tried his patience. And the word 'human' seemed far too sentimental. In truth, though, they were all the same to him and any man could have been sitting in Fab's chair, playing The Game.

Lawrence ignored his food and instead, while he sipped the inferior wine, stared out the window at this fragment of rue Ste. Catherine. The chic restaurant was situated in the heart of the gay ghetto. Many miles of this east-west street formed a potpourri of districts, from poverty, to high commerce, to hooker, to gay, to biker and then to deeper poverty.

"I adore Ste. Catherine's," he said into the glass, thinking how the street reflected his checkered past.

"How?"

He gave Fab a meaningful look. "So many roles, *mon petit bon homme*, so little time. At least it breaks up the *ennui*."

Fab laughed that silly laugh of his. That laugh which had obviously never touched true despair.

Lawrence, as always, picked at his linguini, too indifferent to eat, and the waiter cleared away the remnants with the usual frown and vague open-ended question not really designed to receive a negative response.

"Well, if they hadn't outlawed absinthe...," Fab said, trying, no doubt, to relate.

We'd all be dead, Lawrence thought, and drank the dregs of the sour wine.

"How much worse can it be than chartreuse?" Fab wondered absently. "Speaking of chartreuse..."

He nodded and Lawrence turned toward the door; a tall, blonde drag queen named Luzanne was making An Entrance. "Don't you love it!" Fab laughed like a gleeful child.

"Where did she steal that dress!" Lawrence said, deadpan, but he felt on automatic pilot. He'd said this line, or one just like it, and had heard it so many time...

"Isn't that the chiffon they taped around one of the floats at Gay Pride Day?"

The six foot burly man wore a classic Dolly Parton, sequins, rhinestones, a bosomy second skin in a sickly yellow. His gestures weren't Dolly's, but then he wasn't exactly on stage at the moment. Lawrence, unlike Fab, was bored with DQs. He'd seen too many over what felt more and more like an unnaturally long span on this earth, and they were all alike. He'd even tried drag himself for a while—it lost its glamour quickly, and fucking men in skirts grew tedious. Everything had grown tedious.

They watched Luzanne prance for a while, Fab lacing the air with pithy comments, Lawrence letting his attention wander around the restaurant. Faces, familiar, even the ones he knew he hadn't seen before. Did everyone fit into a 'type'? Hardcore. Precious. Window dressing. Bike Boys. Serious Leather. Transies. The odd Lesbian. A leftover Fag Hag from the 70s. This was worse than a straight restaurant!

"Well, at least she left the Queen's Purse at home this time!" Fab said, and tilted his head in a clownish way.

"Let's get out of here," Lawrence said.

Fab paused, batted his eyes and lifted an eyebrow. "Your wish is my command. What did you have in mind?"

"Your place."

Fab's other eyebrow lifted too. He looked startled. That was good. Catching them offguard was the best.

A dark look passed over Fab's face, or it could have been the shadow of the waiter bringing the bill. Lawrence had never been to Fab's apartment. He'd always avoided it, much to Fab's distress, and then when The Game turned slightly, and Fab had stopped inviting him, Lawrence began saying he wanted to visit. Fab resisted, but his heart wasn't in it, that was clear. It was pushy of Lawrence to bring it up again, since they'd just gone over this ground on the way to the restaurant. But in an instant, he realized he was crushingly bored; it was time to play this out.

Suddenly Fab threw back his head and thrust one shoulder forward, Garboesque. He batted those seductive dark lashes and murmured in a throaty voice, "I vouldn't vant you to be alone!"

Lawrence said nothing, but he felt a vague regret pass through him, which quickly solidified to stone. Yes, it was definitely time to move on.

They walked along the snowy pavement of *rue la Gauchetierre*, past the tall metal staircases and wrought-iron balconies of this solidly French district where Fab lived. He was French, not Québecois, but that was about all he had ever said concerning his background. He didn't like to talk about himself and Lawrence didn't probe; he just wasn't that interested. Lawrence, of course, always lied about his past. They never knew the difference and by the time they realized the falsehoods, it was too late.

"Remember *le Bastille?*" Fab said. More sentimental crap. This was getting better and better. He was alluding to when they met, at the baths six months ago. The attraction was non- physical from Lawrence's end. Sex wasn't important to him, although he'd never had trouble functioning. What interested him more was The Game. And part of The Game involved the build up. And that took time.

But for Fab the attraction was a complex mosaic, and Lawrence quickly learned to play off every motif. He made sure they liked the same clubs, shared a taste for similar movies, and for hairy, good-looking men, which worked out well for maintaining a trouble-free friendship. Every once in a while Fab made noises about fucking him, and Lawrence passed it off as a joke. Then, later, a pointed remark to Fab, that sex between them was out of the question, wasn't it? That the relationship would never go beyond friendship... Then, when Fab seemed distressed enough, resigned, then the come on. A subtle touch here, a comment there. All of it designed to rev Fab up again. And then the questions, prying into Lawrence's fabricated past, the hints, finally the blatant offers, then the rejection. It had been a good Game, going around and around to Lawrence's delight, and had lasted longer than most. But he was tired of it.

They climbed the icy steps to the second floor non-descript door. Inside, they hiked the steep narrow staircase to the third floor. Fab unlocked his door and they entered black space.

"Forget to pay your electric bill?" Lawrence said. But when the lights didn't come on, he fumbled inside his jacket pocket for the lighter.

As the flame came to life, Fab walked around the room striking matches and lighting candles; there were many dozens.

"When did you get into hot wax?" Lawrence said, but Fab didn't reply. It suddenly seemed pressing to Lawrence that he didn't know what Fab did for a living, how he spent his time when they weren't together. That, he suddenly realized, was foolish thinking, and he dismissed such useless thoughts. Better to know nothing about them. It was easier that way.

The candlelight lit the living room in a way that cast shadows everywhere, although Lawrence's own was not visible, which made him feel even more alien than he normally felt. The large space, as with so many Montréal apartments, had a kitchen off one end, and a bedroom off the other. The bathroom, he figured, must be the door next to the apartment door.

Lawrence walked around, gazing at everything as if this were a museum. Religious paraphernalia abounded, icons from a variety of faiths, and even a display of hands with blood prints on the palms. Vampires were the main theme, though, in all shapes, sizes, colors and materials. Bela faces, photographs of Christopher Lee and Gary Oldman, statues of anonymous Draculas, dolls with capes and fangs, all either dangling from the walls and ceilings, or perched on shelves, or hovering menacingly in corners, or craved into the wooden arms of the sofa and poised on the table tops. Besides the obvious theme, another commonality became clear: each face was hideous in its lust and starvation; the overall effect was cheap and tawdry. It made Lawrence feel superior to this tasteless man.

"You've been dying to come here," Fab said, which caused Lawrence to laugh slightly. "So now that you're here, you might as well get comfy."

Fab's voice had turned serious, more serious than Lawrence was accustomed to hearing it, and he wondered if pushing this was a bad idea. He wasn't afraid, just surprised, but he didn't want any complications, especially heavy emotional scenes, now that The Game had come to the end. Fab was so shallow, always up, always lifting the half full beer glass for inspection. For a while, Lawrence had found the contrast between his own sombre nature and Fab's lively of-the-people temperament intriguing; now it just irritated him. Fab was boring. But like so many of the lower-class, he was also prone to melodrama; the vampire-covered walls between this apartment and the next were paper thin.

Lawrence took a seat on a Louie Quatorze chaise, covered in what might have been cheap blood-red velvet. Appropriate, Lawrence thought. "Aren't you going to sit?" he asked Fab. But Fab continued standing in front of him.

"Tell me, Larry, have you always been so dismal?"

Lawrence hated being called Larry, and Fab knew that. But he wasn't going to show it. "You should know me by now." Which, of course, was absurd; Fab didn't know him, would never know him.

"I know you, baby. I've known a lot of men like you."

"Oh please! This isn't going to be the List of Conquests, is it?"

"Not at all. I have nothing to prove. But you do."

Fab seemed to tower above him, confronting him in some way. Lawrence shifted uneasily. He had wanted to enjoy this, drag it out a bit, something to remember later. Maybe fast and furious was better this time. Maybe not. "Opting for melodrama? Listen, what do you have to drink?"

"Why? You never have more than a glass of wine a night. Or eat, that I've seen."

"The little man is observant."

"I've watched you. You just nudge the food around on your plate, and leave beverages sitting there all night—"

"Well, we all want Céline Dion's figure."

"Life doesn't interest you. Been there, done that. You're bored by existence and suck the life out of everybody you come in contact with because you're afraid to die."

Lawrence didn't know what to say. He had been bored, a long long time. But that didn't give Fab the right to fracture his reality. Besides, this was his Game, his rules. "It's not my fault if people are vulgar and deadly dull. Even the lowest creature with sensibilities crawling on this planet would be jaded."

"I'm not."

"You've just proved my point, darling! Give it a rest."

"Watched *The Boys in the Band* one too many times, Larry? You're a walking cliche. Maybe it's time to use the stake on you, move you on, leave a space for others who might find life fascinating."

"Others? You mean, like you? Give me a break! You wallow in everything that's pedestrian, and call it intriguing. You have about as much style as some 2.5 daddy in the burbs!"

How did it get to this? Lawrence wondered. This cusp of intensity. Fab was close to yanking feelings out of him, angry feelings, long buried. God only knew what was behind them! They had never been friends but they were becoming enemies, and that would not do. And suddenly the familiar non-feeling washed over him; he just didn't care. If they argued. If they didn't. He would never see Fab again after this night. Even the knowledge of that left him on the pleasant side of comfortably flat.

Suddenly, Fab dropped to his knees, taking Lawrence totally by surprise. He crawled forward, pressing between Lawrence's legs. Candlelight flickered on his handsome features; he resembled a supplicant in this room full of the relics of faith and faithlessness. His fingers found the belt, unbuckled it, pulled down the zipper, eased down the jeans.

In the darkness, Lawrence smirked. This is how it always went: They wanted it. No, they needed it. And that sealed their doom. Tomorrow Lawrence would be gone, leaving an empty shell behind. But they were all cast from the same mold, these bubble boys. They never fessed up to what they really were about, to be used and abused in ways they couldn't even envision. To be hurt to the core, and left wounded, bleeding to death. That's what turns them on. The ultimate passion, the thing that takes them to the edge and then shoves them over, where they're terrified to go but are nevertheless headed. And Lawrence was the one to take them there. His inhuman coolness attracted them. And these pathetic beings thought he was just struggling to open up!

Fab had Lawrence's cock in his mouth and was working it with emotion, like there would be no tomorrow. And for him, there wouldn't be. The thick lips kissed and sucked lovingly, enthusiastically, just the way Fab did everything. Lawrence felt the pressure in his balls. What Fab would drink would seal his fate. He could not envision such chilling semen. Just as none of the ones before him had been able to envision it either.

Lawrence's only regret, if he had a regret, was that he was never around to see them the next day, devastated, the victims of a callous killer, who nourished himself on souls, not food, and who consumed essence instead of fine wine.

He lay his head back against the chaise. Above, a caped, corpse-like form extended from the wall and leered down at him in the candle-light. The creature was from another realm, a dark and lonely place that he knew so well, that was all he knew. Lawrence stared into its stone-cold eyes as Fab made the frigid juices burst from his cock. And then Lawrence screamed, as he always did when they finally took it from him. The semen pumped until there was nothing more to offer at this alter of vapid existence. Until he was completely drained, and needed replenishing.

It was time to end this, to bring it to its natural conclusion. Lawrence gripped the arm of the chaise hard, and struggled to his feet. The darkness of this candle-lit crypt Fab called home bothered him. And he felt unbearably weak. Oddly, his cock still throbbed. He needed to act fast, before his energy gave out and time did him in.

Fab stood too. His face seemed filled out, as if the cold beverage he had extracted from Lawrence had nourished him. Even his lips were dark in the dim light, and his eyes glittered with life. "Poor puppy," he said, as if he were old and Lawrence just a boy. "You just don't understand life, do you? How important it is to live it."

The room spun. Lawrence sank to his knees hitting something hard, like packed earth. Images flew past his swirling vision, creatures of the darkness come to life to carry him through the door to their realm—had he so long slept on the doorsteps, awaiting entrance?

Blood rushed from his head. How had Fab drained him? And then he knew. The face there, hovering, so full and alive, bloated, lived off *everything* in it's path, indiscriminately. The full, the empty; the successful, the failures; the living and the dead. He embraced all equally, ravishing, continually nourishing himself. Lawrence was a novice player compared to this one, and he suddenly understood with shocking clarity that this time he had gone about The Game all wrong.

"My blood..." he managed, feeling the wet stickiness between his legs, wondering if the words had even left his lips.

They must have, because Fab answered. "Tasty. Refined. Definitely one of the special ones, Larry. But you know, it all ends up in the same place, mixed in here with the rest."

Focusing on Fab's face in the near darkness was nearly impossible. But his eyes said it all. Darkness that fed off darkness and light and expanded, eternally. And what the eyes expressed so eloquently, the two sharp incisors said in a more blatant way: Lawrence was nothing special. Nothing at all.

Against his will, Lawrence's eyelids dropped. His heartbeat slowed. He watched himself pitch forward into a widening chasm. Down below he saw the blood-pool of humanity rise up to embrace him. What he had consumed, he had become. The blood drowned his screams, but not Fab's laughter.

The Hungry Living Dead

At last I have died and gone to Hell, Réjean thought. He paused on the sidewalk, assaulted by the discordant sounds escaping through the cracks in the red brick walls.

This club, like many others he had been to, was located in a run down area of the city, in a structure built about one hundred years ago. Not a particularly creative period architecturally, he thought, but at least it holds a flavor that the modern slabs of concrete and steel piercing the sky lack.

He sighed. They were all alike, these places. Follow the steps down into the chilled earth. Over the worn door with a peephole hangs the inevitable, nearly invisible sign, this one with the word *Sanctuary* burned into a black plastic chevron. Knock and, provided you look the part, they open unto you.

Inside the air was dense and stale, pungent with the odors of sweat, tobacco and a variety of intoxicants. His nostrils stung; his aesthetics were offended. A cacophony of instruments and voices careened off the black walls, impaling all in their path. A tomb for the living, he thought. Dank. Filthy. Hidden. Crawling with repugnant life forms. At least it was dark.

He had come here out of desperation. They possessed blood. The ruby river of life would be tainted with impurities, but he needed it to survive. It was abundant here. And, more importantly, they gave it willingly. Réjean moved to a gloomy corner. He felt dozens of voracious eyes staking his back. His costume fit the purpose: a great coat and pants of velvet, and a silk ascot, all ebony, of course. His shirt glittered knife blade silver. The high calfskin boots were a color light could not penetrate; his heels clicked smartly against the painted concrete floor, but only he could distinguish the sound amidst the noise. A layered cape rested on his broad shoulders, the type he once wore in daylight, when he had walked as one of the living.

These youths loved theatrics, and the outfit, the most flamboyant in the room, attracted them, which was why he wore it. He swung the cape back over one shoulder dramatically, lay the cane with the silver wolf's head tip on top of the small round table and sat. He removed the gloves slowly, for effect, scanning the room with disdain. Even before he draped the leather gloves across the cane, a female stumbled toward him.

Young, barely twenty, emaciated, as most of them were. Dressed in black, from her fashionable Doc Martens, tights, mini-skirt and gothic lace blouse, to the leather jacket she wore, the front studded with safety pins and stainless steel grommets. The back, he knew, would display a grisly picture of a skull, or a fanged version of Murnau's *Nosferatu*. Her scalp was shaved, making her eyes appear very large and liquid. As she neared, he noticed a spider tattooed on one side of her bare head.

Silently he gestured for her to sit. She nearly lost her balance but finally perched on the edge of the chair opposite him. She stared at him and tugged at the dozens of earrings and clips along her left ear. He knew the game perfectly; withholding would force her out. Eventually, she sucked in her generous lower lip, painted mold green, took a drag from a nearly finished cigarette, then blurted, "You look just like Lestat!"

He'd heard this before, of course. Many times. The look was intentional and he had often silently thanked Mrs. Rice for painting such a clear portrait that resembled him. He lay his head back against the wall, lowered his eyelids and stared down his nose at this *fille* in what he knew would convey a taste of the danger she craved. She had seen such looks in vampire movies. She knew how to respond.

The girl moved her chair closer. As she did so, *Interview With the Vampire* fell from her jacket pocket. They both reached down to pick up the worn paperback. Their fingers touched. "You're ice!" she said, shocked. Intrigued. Her breath stank of beer and cigarettes. The dross of other substances seeped from her pores.

"You can melt me," he assured her, his voice floating along the air.

"How?" She took a nervous drag, but only the filter was left. Her eyes glittered.

"I think you know."

He heard her heartbeat quicken and he felt the vibration as strongly as if he held that organ in his palm.

She glanced across the room and gestured wildly to a male sitting at the table she had vacated. He joined them immediately.

Tall, painfully lean, holes in the requisite spots in his black denim pants and tight tank top. A ferret hung over the back of his neck, under his tied-back jet hair. The rat-like animal, sensing danger, scurried beneath the motorcycle jacket.

The male noisily dragged over a chair and sat with them. Réjean inhaled the odor of tart sweat wafting from his body, tinged with an undercurrent of sweet sex. The young man's lashes were stained and lined in black, giving him an androgenous look. His glassy eyes shone intensely, but he was not as intoxicated as the girl.

"Jason, man." The boy held a palm up, thumbs to be hooked in the modern ritual of greeting.

"I am Réjean." He grasped the warm hand and held it; Jason, too, felt the chill. The expression of disbelief on the young face faded to excitement.

"Man, like are you really the undead?"

"Of course." There was no need to hide the truth. So many people drank blood now, every newspaper and magazine, every TV talk show featured stories of real vampires, that Réjean knew he could safely disguise himself as one of these deviants. Whatever these two before him believed was irrelevant. "'For the blood is the life'," he said knowingly, stating clearly his true purpose for being here.

"You got it, man!"

"Hey," the girl pipped up, "tell us about, like, how it was, you know, when you were human and everything. And how you got to be a vampire."

"Yeah, let's hear some stories. You must have been like a prince or something." The young man pulled a plastic box from his jacket, opened it and took out three capsules, which he swallowed. The girl helped herself. The box was offered to Réjean.

He stared at them blankly. They were famished infants, squalling to be fed. And yet even if he could feed them, which he could not, they would never be full. "Perhaps later. After refreshment."

Jason's leg jerked frantically to the music for a few seconds, then he stood, but the girl hesitated. Réjean looked into her starved blue eyes, eyes that had seen so much and yet understood so little. There was nothing there worth capturing. She lived for the night, for death, and normal life was as alien to her as it had become to Réjean. Her hesitation did not stem from fear but *ennui*.

"Like, let's hit the back room," Jason said. "Get up!" He grabbed the girl's arm and she stood, a zombie obeying a command. When they disappeared behind a beaded curtain, Réjean sighed. He picked up his cane and gloves and followed.

The narrow corridor he entered reeked of urine and mildew. It was long and dark, but he used the stray light as a cat would. He passed the only washroom; the door had been torn from its hinges. A girl sat on a toilet seat injecting a powerful substance into her arm while another female knelt between her legs, noisily consuming her juices. The seated girl stared at Réjean as he passed, her sunken eyes brimming with lust and hatred. He could tell from her odors that before morning she would be dead in the truest sense of the word.

Jason was framed by a doorway at the end of the corridor. "In here, man. Nobody'll bother us."

The small, windowless room was empty, except for the paper and broken bottles littering the wood floor. Réjean closed the door and slid the bolt. A yellow bulb on a cord dangled from the ceiling; it was enough for all of them to see by. The girl shivered; no heat reached this desolate vault.

Jason used his boot to scrap clear a space. He began to undress the girl. Her small breasts were round and full, the nipples firm from the chill.

"There is no need for that," Réjean said.

"Whatever, man."

Jason sat on the floor and pulled the half-naked girl down. Réjean stood staring at them, the true children of the night, dead before they had been born, disenfranchised from their rightful inheritance. And yet he envied them. Life was within their grasp, if only they would seize it.

"So, like, where you take it from?" Jason asked.

"Where would you like me to take it from?"

"My cock." The young man grinned lasciviously.

"There is a vein in your neck that will do."

Jason snickered but pulled off his jacket. The ferret leapt into the air, hit the floor, raced into a corner and hid beneath a wadded up sheet of newspaper.

Réjean squatted before them. They both stared at him with the innocence of those jaded to pain. For some reason he felt an urge to nurture them and yet he knew they could not receive what little he had to offer. They needed him to be harsh; it was the only love they understood. And he needed their blood.

The young man's skin was dirty, but Réjean had long ago learned to ignore the unpleasant. He pulled Jason to him. The vein, weak, had been overused, but adrenalin pumping through the slim body helped it plump in a way that provided easy enough access to the coppery treasure it conveyed.

Réjean closed his eyes and his teeth instinctively found the entrance way to hot bliss. Blood coated his mouth and the moment the thick substance slid down his parched throat, he moaned and pulled hard on the ragged wound.

A face flashed before his eyes. The face of someone dear. *Etienne, ten years younger, who so resembled him, laughing, sunlight glinting off his fair hair.*

The boy groaned and Réjean clutched him close. *Etienne embraced him. "Mon frere! Mon ami!" An arm slipped around his neck. Etienne kissed him on both cheeks.* Jason kissed his jaw.

Réjean struggled to take only half of what he needed. To stop now was excruciating, but there was still the girl.

Gently he pushed Jason back until the young man lay on the floor, his eyes closed, his legs apart. His diaphram contracted and expanded rapidly. A hand moved to his crotch, unzipped his pants, took hold of the erection. Réjean had a vague memory of the sensations that must be coursing through the boy. But his own lifeless body could no longer appreciate those delights, and the memory was as cold and dense as the walls of the tomb in which he spent the daylight hours.

The girl was submissive and he decided on second thought to undress her completely. She helped him strip her skirt and tights away. Her slim body, pale as a Death Lily, seemed on the verge of something—opening, closing—he could not be certain. He held her firmly with one arm and ran a hand over her breasts, forcing the nipples to firm from more than the cold. He roved the swells of buttocks, squeezing and pinching until she twitched in a semblance of life in his arms. He slid down her hairy mons and slipped a finger between her legs. The flesh inside was dry and cool, and he stroked her until she heated and moisture flowed over his hand and she moaned softly.

The vein he chose was in her breast, near her heart, at the center of a tattoo of a Black Widow spider. As he bit, her nipples hardened and thrust at him. Her head fell back. She pressed her groin against him in a grinding motion, and he felt or imagined himself stir.

Hot blood swelled within him and another memory crystallized. *Amulette, on a sultry mid-summer's day, the blue lake behind her, waist-length hair lush across her full breasts, his hand gently pushing the hair aside. His lips tasting her warm salty flesh, the bud eager to firm to the worship he offered. She moaned and shivered beneath him. His groin felt heavy and hot. The scent of her fiery sex wafted up to tease his nostrils.*

He sucked harder, clutching the girl to him, struggling to bring life to the memory. As his body was fed, for precious moments the past revived, igniting a ray of hope in his dark existence. *Amulette cried his name over and over. He thrust one last time, impaling her impossibly deep, until their bodies seemed to merge.*

The girl slumped against him at the same moment he could hold no more. Reluctantly he stopped. The memory evaporated.

The girl's face looked soft, dreamy. Her full baby lips had parted as though at last she was ready to receive something from a withholding world. Blood snaked along her breast from the wound, painting her pink bud a scarlet rose.

Looking at the two of them was torturous. They could not appreciate what they had. No matter how bleak their existence, their access to memories, both good and ill, allowed them more than he was capable of. He was full of their life's blood, yet hollow within, unable to seize even his own past. Being with them made him feel impoverished.

To have what they have, what they take for granted...Bitterness cut through him. He had been cheated. He needed to leave before he did them real damage.

He headed toward the door.

"Hey, man, that's some rush. Lemme take yours." Jason struggled to his feet, his body weaving.

"I do not share my blood," Réjean said coldly.

"You do me, I do you. That's the gig."

"You said you'd tell us stories," the girl slurred, her voice whiny. Already her body, ripened at his hands, was losing its fullness, retreating to the familiar, the insensate.

"You do not appreciate what you have and yet you want what is mine?" Réjean felt astonished at such greediness.

"Man, don't upload no bull-babble. It's my turn. Get over here!"

The girl crawled across the floor. She grabbed the hem of Réjean's cape and tugged it. "Come on! You promised you'd tell us about your life and stuff."

He felt repelled by them. It was as though they were intent on consuming everything he possessed, which was so little. They wanted his blood. His memories. His life, if they could get it. Like leeches, they would take from him until what he had was theirs and he was left with nothing.

"Man, I want some of yours, and I want it fast and hard!" Jason was on him, tearing his shirt from his body. The girl yanked the cape from his shoulders. They would drain him if they could and toss away the shell. He did not have much but what he had he must protect.

He lashed out. Jason flew across the room. The boy hit the back wall with a thud. Réjean kicked at the girl. She rolled over and over screaming; he heard glass crunch beneath her body.

Réjean raced from the club and into the black night. He flew through the streets, seeing nothing, terror clinging to him like a nightmare. The cemetery was miles away but he returned hours before sunrise.

His ancient coffin offered a peculiar kind of comfort and the cool stone walls of the crypt kept the world at bay. He lay trembling. Memories had surfaced yet he could no longer recall what they were, or their significance to him, but the longing imbedded within those recollections lingered. A longing that he knew he could never satisfy. He clutched himself, but his hands were cold dead things, the flesh of a corpse. The assurance they provided grew stark: he was alone. He would be alone always. Except in the world of the night, populated by hoards of the ravenous living dead.

Vampire Lovers

"*Ma femme de la Nuit,*
How I crave our intimacies.
I last came to you yesterday evening;
I devoured your offering at once.

    You refresh like a new lettuce, capture the sweet joy of the first spring shallot, comfort and arouse as the taste of a vine-ripened tomato. A fresh *salade jardine* for the mind and nourishment for my eternally-hungry heart..."

"I won't compete," Brian said.

"Who's asking you to?" Jersey laid Gaston's letter on the nighttable. After almost a year together, she thought Brian should have gotten over it. Still, she wondered if she did have too many 'vampire lovers'. In England, Germany, Australia. Gaston in Mamaroneck, New York, and Amanda in Atlanta. And a new one in Yellowknife whose gender she wasn't sure of. The paramour in Osaka had an unpronounceable name.

"Look," Brian continued, "they all know more about you than you know about any one of them. You've never met, you don't even have their home addresses, just postal boxes. Don't you find that a little bizarre?"

"It's the way I want it," she said. The way they wanted it.

    Jersey rolled onto her stomach. Brian ran his index finger down her backbone. His palm slowly rounded one cheek, then rested on the other in a proprietary way. She felt the skin of her bottom being nipped, and she shifted onto her side. "It's harmless," she said. "You knew about

77

my hobby when we met. You thought I was mysterious."

"Hobby?" She felt him lift off the bed. "You mean obsession. And when we met there was only one. Now there are thirteen–"

"Twelve."

"Whatever. You spend all your time writing letters."

"Jealous?" She rolled over. He was slipping into his jeans. She watched his arm muscles ripple in the purple light from the lamp beside the bed. The sheen of sweat coating his chest cast a warm but dazzling glow. Just behind his sandy hair, the poster of darkly sensuous Frank Langella as Dracula caught her eye. Heat spread up the inside of her thighs. Brian turned and the petulant look on his face cooled her.

"Bri, this is my business, not yours. I know you're concerned about me but they're only pen pals and–"

"Not my business?" His lips parted enough to let a tortured laugh escape. The violet light caught the saliva on the two pointed eye teeth that had attracted her when they'd first met. "You're up to your nostrils in letter-writing vampires and I'm supposed to sit back and say, No problem, Jersey, spend all your free time with them. If you were half as passionate with me as you are about these post-card bloodsuckers–"

"They're not vampires. They're people interested in vampirism."

"Perverts."

"Well, I guess I'm a pervert too."

He strode to the wall of books and began yanking out volumes. "Look at this trash! *Crimson Kisses. Lust for a Vampire. Demon Lover...*"

"Give me those. They're collectors items. Irreplaceable."

He held them just out of reach. "Jersey, I'm irreplaceable too."

"What's that supposed to mean."

"It means I won't stand by and do nothing while these creatures drain the very–"

"Even for an actor, aren't you being a bit melodramatic?"

"This is out of hand. Your life's been taken over..." He paused to look at her seriously. "I know I told you I could handle it but things aren't working out. You're going to have to choose. Them, or me."

There was a long, stilted silence while Jersey tried to think her way out of this ultimatum. It ended when Brian threw the books in her direction. The apartment door slammed.

She was stunned. But the sight of her precious paperbacks splayed on the floor prompted her to action. She picked each up and checked for damage. A creased cover. One broken spine. She hated Brian and didn't care if she ever saw him again.

She shelved the bruised books and ran a finger lovingly along the length of the top of eight shelves, home to her collection of three hundred books on vampires. She even had a couple reputedly written by vampires, but they, of course, were 'in' jokes.

She pulled out some fiction favorites: *Vampire's Honeymoon*; *Dracula in Love*; *Vamps* (she adored the pixie-faced vampiress artwork); *In Hot Blood*, with the super erotic cover. She moved down a shelf to more serious works. Massive tomes, some. *Varney the Vampire* or *The Feast of Blood*; *The Vampire, His Kith and Kin*; *The Annotated Dracula*.

The collection ranged from scholarly to pornographic, staid to lurid, quality to trash, and she loved them all irrespective of age or value.

When Jersey finished she went to the full-length bathroom mirror and studied her naked body. Not fat, not thin. Voluptuous covers it, she thought. A kind of Mina Harker hourglass figure. She piled her long chestnut hair on top of her head, pursed her lips and struck a pose, exposing her throat to the glass. Victorian erotica. She giggled and ran a bath.

While soaking in the steamy pink bubbles, Jersey brushed Brian from her thoughts. She concentrated on the letters she owed. She should write Amanda, who was always so impatient to hear from her. And Toshe, her nickname for Toshahamuka. And before the others, Gaston. Gaston, whom she had written to the longest, ever since he answered her ad in a Philadelphia newspaper. Gaston, whose six page letters—she could almost hear his accent—swept her out of the boring and mundane and into another time. He had been born in France, trained as a chef and was a history buff. His ideas and attitudes were as avant garde as any of the late Renaissance men he wrote about. She found his descriptions of dining in Paris in the seventeenth century deliciously tormenting. Jersey imagined him as a Saint Germain figure, and herself a guest at one of his opulent dinner parties, wearing a gold brocade gown bordered in peach tulle and accented with sequined appliques, hair powdered and sculpted into a coquettish style of the day, cleavage brazenly exposed, flirting over the top of an ivory fan. Flirting with Gaston. Although she had no idea what he looked like, her imagination created a suave and charming man about her age with midnight hair and wickedly full lips. His obsidian eyes glinted in a way that warned her he could be dangerous. All the more alluring.

Yes, before any of the others, she must write to Gaston. Immediately. She scooped bubbles onto her neck and massaged them downward and into her swollen nipples.

A week without Brian stretched into three. At first Jersey missed him. She phoned but always got the answering machine and hung up. Once she left a message, on the pretext that she wanted the keys to her apartment back, but he did not return her call. She walked past his house a couple of times; the lights were off and she didn't have the nerve to knock—what if he rejected her again. Jersey gradually replaced longing with keeping busy.

Almost from the moment Brian left, the letters began arriving fast and furious. She could hardly keep up with them. In fact, she suggested to the nearby correspondents—Amanda and Gaston—that they exchange phone numbers with her. Both declined.

When the check finally arrived for the major graphics contract she'd completed last month, Jersey decided she was ready for a vacation. Besides, there was no time left for work. Each day she found at least half a dozen letters stacked in her mailbox. She spent hours reading them, entire afternoons replying to as many as she could and then, on her daily trip out of the apartment, walked to the post office first, the grocery store second and finally stopped at the fantasy and horror bookstore on the way home. After a late dinner she'd watch a movie or two from her vampire video tape collection, read a novel or non-fiction book then crawl into bed around midnight, only to struggle through long and complex dreams she could not recall.

When she first woke each morning, her body was hot and moist and unsatisfied. The bedroom of her small apartment in the unforgiving daylight looked cluttered, dirty, the shelves crammed with too many books and tapes, the walls hidden by garish B-movie posters. Jersey became painfully aware that she was alone. She ached with disappointment. She would fall back against the pillows, sleeping later and later, only getting up when the afternoon shadows magically dampened the harsh glare of reality.

As the intensity of the dreams increased, so did the volume of letters. Sometimes two a day from the same correspondent. It was as if her pen pals had an intuitive sense of her need. The letters became more intimate. Even passionate. But none of the letter writers were as ardent as Gaston.

He teased her, titillated her. He spoke in food metaphor.

"To create *haute cuisine*," he wrote, "a great chef is as a master vampire—he controls the process of transformation.

"*Ma petite* Jersey, should I be permitted the honor of preparing food for you, be warned. I will be demanding! Your hands, I will bind them, your eyes, I blindfold. You must wait patiently, your mouth open and ready, an expression of trust and vulnerability. Then, when the moment arrives, *voila!* I lead you to the appetizer. You linger over the scent as my fork gently braises your tongue. A taste only! Texture. Subtle spicing. The weight of the food within your orifice. Your palate, it will be aroused. 'If only I could have one more forkful,' you sigh, but the soup awaits.

"Ah, the soup! A divine marriage. The plump flesh of mussels and scallops enveloped together in warm, silky cream. A hint of saffron for stimulation and you feel the heat. I describe the earthy, musky taste as the tip of my tongue roams the folds of a mussel. Defiant, you thrust forward aggressively and take from my spoon. Suddenly you are caught in a wave of euphoria, cresting the peak of flavor. But trust me. I shall rescue your palate from desensitization; you will neither reach the mountain top nor rest long in the comfort of the valley between courses.

"The *entrée* torments you. At first you ask politely, may you have just another taste? My denial causes your temper to flare. You become consumed with jealousy, hatred, resentment; I reduce you to tears of joy and frustration. Ultimately you beg, in a frenzy, mad with desire, promising me the impossible, but I remain strong for both our sakes. Together we must contain the tension that threatens to erupt.

"As I present a luscious dessert, you are swollen with longing. My final creation stimulates you beyond what you imagine you can endure to a hunger that is both excruciating and exquisite. You cry out, a moist, succulent fruit, bursting with ripeness, pleading to be plucked...

Ah, Jersey, how we will feast together on *le repas ravissant.*"

She wanted to meet him, but Gaston refused. There was only one option.

Jersey had never been to Mamaroneck, a bedroom community of New York City in Westchester County. Wave after wave of stoic old homes and repressed suburban duplexes passed by as she drove along Mamaroneck Harbor. Library Lane wasn't a long street and she had no trouble finding the right number. She rechecked the address and looked up.

UNITED STATES POST OFFICE.

Just inside the building was a row of neat stainless steel postal boxes. "The numbers only go to 300," Jersey said to a humorless woman at the stamp counter.

"That's right."

"Where can I find 4514?"

"You can't."

"But I send letters to that box all the time. And I get replies from the person I write to so they must be getting the mail."

"Got the right post office?" The woman began adding up a column of numbers.

Jersey had brought all Gaston's letters along. She read the addresses in the upper left-hand corners. Each said Box 4514. Anyway, she'd been writing to him long enough to know it by heart. "Look, something's wrong here. It must exist. If it doesn't, where do the letters go?"

The woman lifted her hand from the calculator momentarily and thumbed over her shoulder. Jersey looked at the room behind the clerk. There were desks and tables piled with boxes and envelopes going out and slots filled with the same, presumably that had come in and were waiting to be delivered. "The door. By the water cooler."

Jersey walked to a small gate and the woman at the wicket, still without looking up, buzzed her through.

The door had a frosted glass window with *Private* stencilled in gold letters. She knocked lightly, then louder, and tried the knob.

Inside the cramped space an officious-looking man, tiny, tight-lipped, wearing wire-rimmed glasses that had been popular in the 60s, probably when he was young, sat behind a wooden desk. He scowled upward and said, "Yes?" not too warmly.

Her heart sank. Thoughts washed through her brain as waves of agonizing disappointment hit emotionally. This couldn't be Gaston.

The man tapped the eraser end of his pencil rapidly onto an old-fashioned blotter and glanced at his watch.

"I...I was told to see you," she stammered, hardly knowing what to say. "The postal box."

"Do you want to rent one?"

"No. I'm looking for a particular box."

"And what box would that be?"

She gave him the number and watched a knowing look cross his face. His lips twisted into a strained and grotesque smile. He lay the pencil down. "You must be Jersey Lawrence."

As she'd feared. This constricted little man was her handsome and sexy Gaston. She swallowed hard, forced a smile and stuck out a hand. "Yes. Nice to meet you."

He did not take her hand. "I've been sending you letters for a year now."

"And I appreciate the correspondence."

"If you appreciate it so much, why haven't you stopped writing, like any normal person would have."

"Stopped writing? But I thought you liked—"

"Young lady, for over twelve months you've written to a postal box that does not exist. I've returned your letters and even written you myself, to no avail. You are either pathologically lonely or mad as a hatter. Why do you keep writing when your mail ends up at the Dead Letter Office?"

As Jersey drove home, she felt shattered. According to Mr. Daniels, (that was his name), Gaston was no more a reality than his postal box. Daniels speculated that somehow the letters returning to her had been intercepted, but in fact she got the feeling he thought she was crazy. All he knew for certain was that he kept returned her letters, along with his own letters to her, and that she kept writing.

When Jersey reached her front door, letters overflowed the box and littered the porch. She picked one up. The grey envelope was from Gaston; more food erotica. She was furious.

She had spent the drive back figuring out that Brian must be behind this. They'd met just after the first correspondences. He told her he had once worked as a cook. As an actor he could easily play the part of different characters on stage; his talents obviously extended to writing. He traveled a lot; buying foreign postage stamps and having rubber stamps made up to cancel them wasn't difficult. Her mailbox was outside; it would be easy enough to steal the returned letters and write replies. There was no one else it could be but she failed to see a motive. She went to his place to confront him.

Jersey climbed to the porch of the hundred year old Victorian house and rang the bell. The last sunlight glinted off the bay window as she peered inside. Brian's spotless stainless steel kitchen, at the front of the house, looked dark and empty.

After she tried the bell again and knocked, she turned the knob, surprised when the door opened. "Brian?"

The air was a bit stale. She walked through the kitchen to the dining room then the living room at the back. Everything was neat and orderly, the way Brian liked it. She ran a finger over the CD player; it was coated with a fine layer of dust. Not like Brian at all.

Upstairs she checked his office, the bathroom and, the bedroom. There something felt off. The sunlight had faded but she didn't want to turn on a light. Brian's king-size futon was made up with the black and grey comforter she'd helped him pick out. At first glance everything appeared normal. Then she realized what was missing. The picture of her and Brian together that he kept on his dresser was gone. Despite the anger, Jersey felt hurt.

She opened the top drawer. There it was, face down. She lifted the picture out. The glass inside the nickel frame was cracked in four places, as though it had been damaged intentionally. The drawer also contained stacks of letters, addressed to her various vampire-lover correspondents, Jersey's return address in the upper corner of the envelope.

"Find what you're looking for?"

She jumped at the sound of his voice. The picture slid from her hands and what was left of the glass shattered irrevocably. "Brian. I... The door was open."

"I've been expecting you."

He looked pale in the dim light. And angry.

"Can we turn on the light?" she asked, feeling nervous, but he didn't move.

She went to the wall to flip the switch herself but he caught her wrist; his hand felt icy. "Let me go," she demanded.

He forced her backwards onto the bed. Then he was on her.

"I know you wrote those letters!" she yelled.

"You do, do you? And have you figured out why?"

"Yes. You wanted to make me look like a fool."

He let her go and sat up. She watched him in the growing darkness. He rested his elbows on his knees and bent his head to his hands. His voice was low. "Your ad intrigued me. It seemed too good to be true—a woman interested in the shadowy side of life. Interested in vampires. After we began writing I managed to meet you and still keep writing but from the start you seemed disappointed with the flesh and blood me. The only thing that brought you alive was vampires—as long as they were on paper or in print. I thought if I could keep you excited, through the letters, maybe that passion would filter into our relationship and..." He turned to her, a dark form in a darker world. "I was wrong on two counts. I deceived you. And you wouldn't give up the others."

She pulled his body onto hers. His weight in the gloom, the delicious texture of his cool skin, his pungent scent, she took it all in. "Kiss me," she whispered. His lips slid over hers hungrily. Someone's teeth—hers, his—cut into the plump skin of her lips and she tasted salty blood. "Bite me again," she pleaded. He lifted up to look at her in the dark, his eyes black diamonds. She arched her throat and his lips did not hesitate to press down onto it. Two sharp points nicked her delicate skin. "Just a little," she groaned.

With one hand he captured her wrists above her head. Her body became liquid fire, but he took his time, savoring the blood, tasting only a little. From here. From there. Teasing her. With each small piercing she cried out for more yet afraid she would go insane from desire.

Just before sunrise he took her. She was moist and swollen, a ripe fruit begging to be plucked.

Mythological & Historical Revenants

In Memory Of...

If memory serves, yellow marigolds and blue narcissus clotted the flower beds of my father's estate in Clontarf that August. The gardener had outdone himself, and it was as though at every turn, life itself permeated the grounds—short-lived life. But 1875 was the spring of my years. Barely seventeen and dreamy, the way Irish girls were then, my future stretched before me like an endless bare canvas, awaiting whichever colors and brush strokes I deigned to paint upon it. Had I but known the outcome of that fateful afternoon, surely I would have fled to the bluffs, hurled my young body over the cliffs and onto the jagged rocks below.

The lawn party my parents hosted was not as large as some, but the *crème de la crème* was in attendance. I recall gazing from the terrace, across the clipped lawn, at the finely attired men in their frockcoats, and the women in soft silks hidden beneath frilly parasols to ward off the sun's rays. Suddenly, for some unknown reason, I gazed upward. A flock of ravens swarmed overhead, so thick that they shrouded the sun's rays, darkening the sky temporarily, sucking up all the light from it. The sight sent a chill down my spine, as if this were a terrible omen of some sort. Just as quickly, that gloomy manifestation evaporated, like a nightmare on awakening, leaving behind only a wisp, a remnant. Immediately the sky brightened.

"May I present my daughter." My father's voice startled me, and I turned. "Florence, this is Mr, Oscar Wilde. Mr. Wilde is a writer, in his first year at Oxford."

"How very nice to meet you." The words caught in my throat, and

I extended my gloved hand.

His face was almost an anachronism. Long, large-featured, flesh pale yet ruddy, with emotion-laden eyes and a peculiar twist at the corners of his full lips. The exact nature of the crooked line between those lips was, for some time, a mystery to me. And what I often felt then to be a grimace, I have now come to understand to be something entirely more sinister.

Mr. Wilde took my hand in his and kissed it, in the continental fashion. "Lieutenant-Colonel Balcombe, your daughter is both remarkably beautiful and, I can see already, utterly charming in a way which will shatter many hearts, all of which, no doubt, will be exceedingly eager to be broken."

I, of course, blushed at such a forthright yet backhanded compliment from this man so startlingly overdressed in a lilac- colored shirt with a large ascot clinging to his throat. If truth be known, more than anyone else, he resembled George the IV, which made me smile secretly—what the French would have called *joli-laid*. His countenance was singularly mild yet his expression ardent. He spoke rapidly, in a low voice, and enunciated distinctly, like a man accustomed to being listened to. Yet beyond all that, his eyes arrested me. I'd never seen such wild intensity, juxtaposed with fragile sensitivity. To this day, try as I might, I simply cannot recall their color, which makes no sense, considering how strongly they held me. What I do recall is that they seemed to capture my very essence, as surely as if my dear soul were a butterfly, suddenly enslaved in a net. A delicate creature destined to be pinned to a board.

My father was called to greet another arriving friend, leaving me to the mercy of this peculiarly enticing stranger.

"There is nothing like youth," he said, in a theatrical manner, gesturing lavishly, speaking loudly, attracting the attention of those standing nearby, yet holding my eye as if it were me alone to whom he spoke. "Youth has a kingdom waiting for it. To win back my youth...there is nothing I wouldn't do..."

I, of course, laughed at such melodrama. "Surely you know nothing of wanting your youth back. My guess, from your appearance, is that you are all of two and twenty."

"From appearances, your guess is nearly correct, less the two. Youth is not merely a chronological order of years, but more a state of mind.

The life that makes the soul, mars the body."

"How strange you are!" I blurted, then felt my face flame. After all, I hardly knew this man, and had not the familiarity with which to taunt him. But he took it in good humor.

"More peculiar than you at present can know. However, Florence, may I call you Florrie?"

"Well, yes, if you like—"

"I do like! Florrie, you must permit me to escort you to church this coming Sunday for the afternoon service."

Flustered, flattered, I could only stumble over my words. "Well...of course. I would be delighted to have you attend our simple country chapel—"

"Excellent! The day is too bright, not the proper setting for a man to offer attention to a woman."

"And church is?"

"One's virtues either shine or dim when the virtuous speak."

With that he kissed my hand again and was gone.

I recall standing, looking down at my hand, which felt as if burning ice had dropped onto it. Then I looked up. My eyes scanned the crowd of my parents' friends. Oscar Wilde had disappeared.

"Tell me about your work, Mr. Wilde." We walked, his hand cupping my elbow, guiding me through the tall rock-strewn grass down the hill toward the rectory, and the chapel beyond, my parents not far ahead of us. I admit that this contact proved thrilling to my girlish body. My affections had already begun swaying in his direction, which, of course, both of us knew.

"My name is Oscar Fingal O'Flahertie Wills Wilde, but you may call me Oscar."

So formal a response made me laugh.

This caused him to glance down at me and frown slightly. "Is that mockery I hear?"

"Mockery, no. Amusement, Oscar. You are so serious. How do you get on in society?"

"I suppose society is wonderfully delightful. To be in it is merely a bore. But to be out of it simply a tragedy. But you were inquiring as to my work."

"Unfortunately, I have not had the chance to read you as yet, although I'm certain you must be a fine poet and will go on to be an excellent writer of prose."

"You are either foolish or perceptive, but, of course, I favor the latter. And what do you know of poetry?"

"I know that it is a taste of God's passion."

"Poets know how useful passion is. Nowadays a broken heart will run to many editions."

"You speak of broken hearts on such a beautiful summer's day? Have you survived one?"

"A poet can survive everything but a misprint."

"You're not very forthcoming, are you, Oscar?"

He stopped walking and turned toward me. I felt my heart flutter. The air seemed to encase the two of us.

"Florrie, all art is quite useless. Before you stands a shallow man, make no mistake about that. One in need of a muse who will inspire him beyond mere banality. More, nourish him."

Words escaped me. I knew not what to answer, or if an answer was at all required. I only knew that we seemed to stand there for an eternity. And as we stood together, locked in an embrace, his eyes drew me until I felt myself dimming, willingly. I knew in those moments I would offer up to him whatever he needed, whatever he wanted.

"Miss Balcombe. It is so nice to see you. And may I enquire, who is your friend?"

The voice of Reverend Sean Manchester broke the moment. Suddenly it was as though I'd been under a spell. I felt stunned, aware that I'd not heard the birds or felt the intense heat for some time. But rather than perceiving the good Reverend's voice as a lifeline, cast toward a drowning swimmer, I felt it an intrusion. With some effort, I forced myself back to the surface of the waters known as reality.

"Reverend Manchester, may I introduce Mr. Oscar Wilde. You will have heard of him, no doubt. He is an aspiring poet, who has already had work published."

"Indeed. I have heard much."

"And I'm certain you shall hear more in future. There is only one thing in the world worse than being talked about," Oscar said, "and that is not being talked about."

The two men shook hands, but perfunctorily. I was dismayed at this adversarial climate between them. I knew it could not be me, for after all, Reverend Manchester was an older gentleman, married a number of years, with several nearly grown children. I could not have known at the time the entirety of this wedge, but I soon had an inkling of its nature.

"You are a young man and already famous throughout the British Isles."

"Don't you mean infamous?"

"Infamy implies sin."

"There is no sin except stupidity."

"If you believe not in sin, I presume then that you also give no credence to conscience."

"Conscience and cowardice are really the same things."

"Then, sir, in your opinion, why do men go astray?"

"Simply, temptation. The only way to get rid of a temptation is to give in to it, it seems to me."

"Oscar!" I felt compelled to interject a note of sanity, for things had got out of hand. Even a poet should respect a man of the cloth. "Surely you believe in salvation! You were raised a Christian, were you not?"

At this, he turned to me again. A small, crooked smile played over those lips, and his eyes again compelled me to focus on him exclusively. That same potent pull threatened to overwhelm me, although his words kept me from sinking. "Florrie, dearest, we are all in the gutter, but some of us are looking at the stars."

"Heaven might be a better destination," Reverend Manchester said, "although there is an alternative."

"And that, I presume, is Hell. Well, Reverend, I have visited that place and not, I suspect, for the last time. I have found it wanting."

Reverend Manchester said nothing more, but the look in his eyes spoke volumes. The church bells were tolling madly, the service about to begin. "I must attend to my parishioners," he said perfunctorily, and, almost as an afterthought, "It is good we have met, Mr. Wilde."

"Yes. A man cannot be too careful in the choice of his enemies."

Reverend Manchester looked startled by this blatant statement. But in my eyes, Oscar had merely said what was evident—the two men did not see eye to eye, although I should have thought 'enemy' too strong a word.

Reverend Manchester excused himself. Oscar turned to me. Before I had the chance to collect my thoughts, he grasped my shoulders and quickly pressed his lips to mine. I was shocked. Embarrassed. Titillated. I scanned the small group of parishioners; none had seen this outrageous act, including my parents, thank God!

When I looked again at Oscar, all of this evident on my face, no doubt, something strange occurred. The contrast between us struck me. His face had become ruddy, while I felt light-headed and pale. He seemed sure of himself, whilst I, on the other hand, had been knocked entirely off balance. As I stared at him, time became irrelevant. The importance of my life seemed to diminish in my mind. The call of my soul's high longings became faint to my ears. A peculiar image came to me: I was composed of tiny particles which normally adhere together as a solid but were now being separated by some invisible dark force. And then, there was only Oscar.

"I must be off, Florrie," he said.

"What? You're not attending the service?" I heard my voice as if from a distance. Who is asking this question? I wondered. And who pretends to care for the answer?

"I have other plans. Permit me, though, to call on you this week."

It wasn't exactly a question, but more of a statement he made. And before I could respond, he turned and was gone.

I know that Reverend Manchester's sermon focused on the devil, finding him here and there, and being on guard, but I could only concentrate on snatches of what was said. You see, I was already in love. At least, I called it love then, but I have since learned to identify it as indenture. Bits of my soul were siphoned from me that day and what would occur afterwards would make a normal woman grieve for a lifetime. But already I had ceased to be normal and even my gender became inconsequential to me. And I was incapable of grief.

Oscar visited my home twice a week for two weeks. After that, he became a permanent fixture in our parlour. Nightly, mother, or my auntie, chaperoned, as was the custom then. Neither approved of him— Oscar was not an ordinary man. I was only too eager to assure them that he was, in fact, a genius, destined for great things. They would have none of it.

"You can't be serious!" Auntie chided me. "What kind of a husband do you think a man wearing a purple great coat would make!"

"Style," I informed her, "is not a paramount concern, although his dress is avant garde, in my opinion."

"Your opinion," Mother said, "hardly matters here. You're but seventeen years of age. Need I remind you that your father and I make your decisions as long as you reside under our roof? This is not a match made in heaven."

"But it is not made in that other place either, Mother. Were you never young once? Did your heart not rule you when Father was near?"

"My head superseded my heart, or at least the heads of your maternal grandparents. Fortunately, their clearer minds prevailed. You are seeing entirely too much of Mr. Wilde."

"You're young, child," Auntie declared. "There are other suitors, more worthy."

In the way of youth, I created a scene, as they say, and left them both standing there speechless. But it was as though I watched my antics, disconnected. Then, of course, I interpreted my reaction to being overly intimidated at vexing my elders with my disrespectful behavior.

Time has proven auntie's word both right and wrong—incorrect in the context of her meaning, but correct in a broader meaning, for I have been loved by at least one other man, much to his detriment.

Mother remained adamant, but Father, however, admired Oscar, and could see that his name would be remembered through the ages. Although, being my father, and concerned with my interests, he was not particularly comfortable with Oscar's financial situation. Unfortunately our family fortunes had taken a turn for the worse—I was dowerless, and, in Mother's words, must count on a "strong pecuniary match". Oscar, you see, was a spend-thrift. His inheritances and endowments were few and far between, and his wants exceeded his resources throughout his life. He spent much too freely, on both himself and his friends. And on me. At Christmas of that year, Oscar presented me with a token of his affections.

Inside the exquisite sculpted shell box of ivory I found a tiny cross. I held it up by the chain and the illumination from the gas lamp seemed to make the gold sparkle. I became mesmerized by that sparkle, and only Oscar's voice returned me to the room.

"Wear this in memory of me," he said, as though he were dying.

On one side was an inscription, uniting our names. My eyes must have shown what was in my heart.

"Florrie," he said ardently, grasping both my hands, falling to one knee before me, in the presence of Auntie, who instantly paused in her needlework.

"I am too happy to speak," I told him. "You must speak for both of us."

I expected a proposal of marriage, although I knew that while he was still a student, marriage was forbidden him. I would have been satisfied with a profession of undying love. But Oscar, in his theatrical manner, while Auntie gazed on, said something entirely unexpected.

"The worst of having a romance of any kind is that it leaves one so...unromantic. You have, of course, won my heart."

And that was that.

Father and Mother, though, on hearing of this incident, took it seriously, although there had been no commitment elicited. They proceeded to check more deeply into Oscar's fiscal, and also personal affairs. Unsavory rumors were alluded to, but my parents refused to provide to me the details.

"Then they are only rumors," I said stubbornly, "whatever their nature. I believe it is unchristian-like to lower oneself to pay credence to mere hearsay."

Mother looked angry. "Now you're beginning to speak as rudely as he."

Father merely raised an eyebrow.

I took a deep breath. "I intend to marry Oscar Wilde!"

"Nonsense!" Mother laughed.

"And has he proposed?" Father wanted to know. "Because he has not as yet spoken with me."

"I know he will," I assured them, although I did not feel completely certain of this. I felt in my heart that Oscar loved me—for he said he did, or so I thought—and what I felt with him erased that horrible feeling of disconnection which became stronger and stronger each day. But the actual words which lead to a vow went missing.

My persistence forced my parents' hand.

"Then you will wish to know, Miss," Mother said in her crispest voice, "that your intended has been seen in Dublin."

"Well, of course. He was in Dublin just last month, which you know as well as I do."

"How impertinent you have become! What I know, which you are about to discover, is that Oscar Wilde was spotted dangling on his knee a woman known as Fidelia."

"Scandalous lies!"

"And further, Mrs. Edith Kingsford of Brighton has offered to intercede on his behalf with the mother of her niece Eva in arranging a match."

I'm certain that the look on my face betrayed my heart. Disassociated though I was, a feeling of being crushed overcame me. That after one year together, Oscar saw fit to toy with my affections seemed impossible, and yet...

Without apology or excuse, I raced from the room. I could not bear to hear more. I tried to deny to myself what my parents told me, and yet when I went over details, little incidents rose from memory. Despite his attentions toward me, I was not blind. Oscar flirted outrageously with every young woman in his sphere. And, since I was facing fact, I had also to acknowledge to myself that he paid equal attention to young men.

When next he visited over the holidays, I was cool to him. His inquiries as to my emotional state brought evasion on my part. "I shan't argue with you," I assured him.

"It is only the intellectually lost who ever argue," he declared.

"Must you always speak as if these are lines from your writings?"

"But they are, Florrie. What can life provide but the raw materials for art."

"I should think that life might be a bit more serious to you."

"Life is too serious already. Too normal. Don't you find it so?"

"And what's wrong with normal? God. Family. Work. Those are what life is all about."

He paused at that. "Fate has a way of intervening in what otherwise would be normal."

I looked at him seriously. "Oscar, I refuse to engage in a battle of witty repartee with you. You have broken my heart."

I waited, but his reply at first was silence. His eyes seemed to sparkle yet were, at the same time, imbedded with impotent sorrow, the latter catching me offguard.

Auntie was, of course, in the parlor with us, although the hour was late and she must have been exhausted—when I glanced across the room, she was dozing by the window.

Oscar, it seems, had observed this also. We sat side by side on the loveseat before the fire. He moved closer and his arms encircled me. I cannot express the apprehension laced with arousal that filled my being. The silence in the room felt like a vise, holding me tightly in its grip, as tightly as Oscar's arms held me. Heat blazed through my body, as if I'd fallen into the fireplace; incineration threatened.

I recall noticing his lips as they came toward mine, twisted into a shape I can only describe as portraying cynicism. I felt both horrified and kindled, but I could not turn away. As his mouth found mine, I experienced a peculiar sensation, as if the breath from my body were being sucked from me. I know I began to panic, arms attempting to flail, legs kicking, noises coming from me. And then I watched helpless as blackness rushed toward me. In a moment of some hellish truth, I recognized that the universe itself was simply empty, Godless, friendless, a place so hollow that love had no reason to exist. And then, I remembered nothing more until I stood at the door, saying farewell to Oscar.

"So, this is goodbye," he said cheerfully, as though it were a happy occasion. I struggled to feel something, and yet I felt numb.

"Have a good trip back to England," I managed. "And be well. You will always be in my heart." The last was not something I felt, but something that came to me, like words on a piece of paper, as though they had no connection to either myself or the situation.

"Ah, but Florrie, you have no heart," Oscar laughed. "At least not anymore." His voice was cold. And while the emotional impact escaped me, by dear body felt the attack and shuddered. In that moment, I recognized my fate. My essence had been taken from me and I would forever be vacant.

I did not hear from Oscar for two years. My parents had finally found a match for me of which they approved. He was an Irishman, of good breeding, a civil servant with ambitions to be a writer. Oscar, in his theatrical manner, sent a letter on hearing of my engagement. He declared that he was leaving Ireland, "probably for good", so that we might never have need to set eyes on one another again. He demanded that I return the golden cross, since, he stated, I could never wear it again. He would keep it in memory of our time together, "the sweetest of all my youth," he said. I could not help but picture that cynical twist to his lips as I read without passion this melodramatic epistle. I kept the cross.

The man I married was a giant, handsome enough, an athlete, an avid storyteller, but was never the good provider Mother had hoped for. In that way he was like Oscar. And in one other. His literary aspirations drove him to write for both the theater, and for print. Since I'd always entertained the notion of acting, once he discovered this, he endeavoured to win me over; I enjoyed a short career on the stage and made my theatrical debut in a play written by my husband. On opening night, I received an anonymous crown of flowers, death-white lilies—I knew they had been sent by Oscar. That was just his style.

I need not reiterate my own marital history. Because my husband obtained a modicum of fame in his lifetime, all of the 'facts' of our life together are a matter of record. The birth of our son Noel. The various tragedies of my husband's professional life, and a scattering of successes. His illnesses, one of which led to his death. The fact that he left me exactly £4,723. Suffice it to say that outwardly our lives appeared normal, at least for those who travel in theatrical and literary circles. But a part of me went missing, and my husband was keenly aware of this lack. And, he knew the source. I told him. It consumed his spirit as surely as my own had been swallowed.

As to Oscar Wilde, over the years I watched him ingest the souls of others—the poor woman he eventually married, Constance Lloyd, and Lord Alfred Douglas, the man with whom he had a lifetime affair, but two of the many whose lives were altered irrevocably. Indeed, Oscar portrayed himself accurately enough in *The Picture of Dorian Grey*. You have likely read the accounts of his life. As always, he sums himself up best: "I was made for destruction. My cradle was rocked by the Fates." Had I but the fortitude, I might have felt some compassion for his trials and tribulations. And in the end, when Robert Ross wrote that macabre account of Oscar's death, describing how 'blood and other fluids erupted from every orifice of his body', I could view the words with but a scientific interest. Oscar had left me incapable of compassion. Nay, incapable of all feeling.

Try as he might, my loving husband could not overcome the damage caused by Oscar Wilde. And although I failed as a wife, still, in at least one regard I inspired my husband; his greatest work will live on, of that I am convinced, even as the works of Oscar Wilde seem to cling to life from beyond the grave. I have sworn it to myself that I will preserve my husband's memory and protect his works to the end of my life—it is the very least I can do.

My husband was more than an insightful man, he was intuitive. If you have not as yet, perhaps you will eventually hear of him and the dark novel which depicts, in metaphor, the agony of the hollow existence of the woman whom he held dear, whose very soul had been absorbed for the refreshment of a psychic vampire.

    A Personal Reminiscence,
      by Florence Balcombe Stoker
        Widow of Irish Writer Bram Stoker
        1925

Memories of
el Dia de los Muertos

———»•»-o-«•«———

You call me death bringer, as though ancient words can wound me. When I was mortal, as you are still, that name filled me with loathing. Now, because I live forever, because I have seen your grandparents rot and will watch *los Gusanos* devour your children, your words fade like the ghosts of memories.

This eve of the Day of the Dead—my day, although you do not yet realize there are many ways to be dead—I watch you enter the cemetery just after sunset. The crude wooden crosses as well as those of fine marble are draped with fragrant marigolds and gardenia and you add your flowers to the stones you stop beside. I see your wife spread a colorful blanket over the graves of your ancestors and open jars and boxes for the long night of sharing. A night when the dead will consume the spirit of the food you offer. Food you expect to devour.

Your son and two daughters pulse with life. Life I no longer possess. They skip along the dusty paths eating sugar skulls and clutching papier-mache skeletons until the sky blackens and the few fires scattered throughout the graveyard become the only light under a moonless sky. The children fall silent and huddle near you, fearful, expectant. You tell them a story. Of how the dead, on this Day, return to converse with the living. To fulfil promises and offer guidance. To bring good fortune. As you play your guitar and sing a song, your eyes are sad and fearful. Years have passed since you have visited the dead. Few still come here to spend the night.

By the flickering embers you stare at the worn oval photograph of your mother and imagine her returning. You want this yet fear it. To speak with her again, to feel her bless you and the ones you love... Your son and daughters have fallen asleep. Your wife is drowsy. She leans back and closes her eyes, her long black hair and the crucifix she wears falling away from her throat. You are alone.

Outside the cemetery walls the *mariachi* band has stopped playing. A cool wind caresses you, blowing hair up the back of our head, exposing your neck. You shiver. I laugh, and you turn abruptly at the sound. Familiar. Alien. Darkness presses in on you and the dead beneath you struggle to call a warning, but their voices were silenced long ago by the worms. You look again to the picture of your mother, then to the sky, and cross yourself, sensing she can no longer help you.

Something flies through the night air, beyond the illumination of the fire. A bat, you hope. Wings flap and you listen as though to a voice. The tequila bottle is less than half full; you take another swallow and I can see you are wondering how you will endure this night.

Once, long ago, when your ancestors and I walked in daylight together, I sat where you sit now. Honoring the dead. Singing sad and joyous songs to them. Telling their tales of grief and bitterness and of how they loved. Of how they lived, and died. Memories stir in me like petals rustled by a breeze.

At last you see me, a shadow among shadows. The guitar slips from your hands. I have come for you. Your eyes are red- rimmed with the knowledge. You plead. Your wife, you say, and your children. There are things you have not yet done. You beg me to spare you until morning, imagining I do not know my powers will wane with the sun. I laugh as tears spill down your weathered face. I am incapable of pity. When I reach out to stroke your cheek, to feel the warmth pushing against your flesh, salty wetness coats my dead fingers. Astonished, I remember.

On a Day of the Dead such as this, when I sat where you sit now, my loved ones beside me, music floating on the cool breezes drifting down from the mountains, I, too, wept. My vulnerable tears betrayed me then, as yours betray you now. My tears did not save me.

What warms your body will soon warm mine. I nod at the boy child, the youngest. A substitute. You decline, as I knew you must. I do not see this as heroism or bravery, simply what you would do.

You turn to the picture of your mother. She will intercede, you think. You pray to her. To anyone. A small iguana springs onto the tombstone next to the melting candle you have placed there. He pauses to stare at you; he is a sign, you believe, good or ill, how can you be certain? I step into the firelight. Neither the dead nor the living can help you now.

"Why?" you ask me. This question I have heard many times over the years. Many times. It is a question for which there is no answer. Your life does not mean to me what it means to you. I feel no love or sympathy, no pity; I no longer understand remorse. All I can tell you is that I long for your hot blood to swirl through my cold body. Your eyes are the only reflection I am capable of seeing and in them I find myself as I once was but am no longer. This image cannot sway me. What I need I must have.

You suddenly understand a horror that all your life you had avoided. You find this incomprehensible: dead exist to whom you mean nothing. And yet even you must know that blood is all that matters on this day when *los Muertos* are honored.

Across the graveyard another calls his ghosts and I listen, intrigued by the bitter-sweet song. The night is long; there are many here with offerings. Many. To one such as myself, all are equal.

Before I turn away, I glimpse disbelief in your eyes. Gratitude. You cross yourself and fall on your knees before your mother. Before me.

I drift between the worn stones toward new warmth. You are a memory already fading. A memory that will die. A memory of the dead.

The Mountain Waits

Like all the others in this village, I was born at the foot of this mountain, lived beside it all my life. The villagers are a simple people, who ask no questions and accept what fate accords them. I bore a child here, buried my parents. That rising earth is our immortal mother, whose body we come from and into whose arms we will return one day. The blood flowing through our veins is one blood, and we pulse as one being. We, and the mountain.

I have always been considered too bold. I have paid a price for being different and my isolation has kept me lonely. But because I am daring, I am the only one who knows what happened up on the mountain top.

Tonight is Halloween. It is like the last Halloween, and the one before that and so on, back into the mists of time. Children from the village who have turned twelve since the previous All Saints' Eve dress up in costumes, but they don't know why. They don't ask. And anyway, the history of the ritual is lost, probably forever, shrouded the way the peek of the mountain is constantly obscured by low-hanging clouds. All the children know is that enough fabric must drape from their shoulders to imitate wings. Hair must be flowing. Their bodies must be naked. The children walk in single file up the path to the top of the mountain. There they wait until midnight of All Hallow's Eve, huddled together where the roads cross. Alone. Without adults. In the morning they all return. All but one.

Each year it's the same. Each year no one questions. And no one talks about what they've seen. And nothing unusual happens. Except for once. Twenty years ago, when I went up the mountain.

That All Hallow's Eve was cold. We'd already had the first frost, killing the tomatoes, damaging the remaining beans. The sun had set hours before. The sky was black with not even a moon yet. Nothing in the fields could be distinguished from anything else. It was as if ebony paint had spilled from the sky, coating everything, devouring all light.

"Renata, time to get ready," my mother said.

I turned from the window I'd been staring out. My mother's hair was turning grey. Her face was worn, the lines etched from constant work and worry. Those lines seemed deeper that night. My father sat in the corner smoking his pipe, staring at the fire in the fireplace. He was silent, as he was every evening after the sun had set.

My mother used the black muslin left over from my grandmother's funeral six months before. The structure of the wings had been made just after the sun dropped down over the horizon, as tradition dictates: bend and twist two wire coat hangers until they arch and curve properly, then bind them together with bailing twine. Once they were affixed to my shoulders with more twine, my mother began fitting the inky fabric, cutting here, stitching there, working methodically as she had done with each of her eight children. I was the youngest, the baby; it was the last time she would do this work.

"I don't see why she has to go," my father said, not daring to put this out as a question—that would have been too frightening for him. Puffs of smoke rose steadily into the air. I watched them drift towards the ceiling and dissipate as if they had never existed.

Each of my sisters and brothers had gone before me, up the mountain. Most of them had returned. One did not. That was Tomas, the eldest. Of course, I hadn't been born yet, but I'd heard the stories. Not of what happened to him, or of why he did not return, but stories of who he was, who he might have been.

My mother didn't bother to reply, just said to me, "Hold still." My father continued to smoke. The clock that sat on the mantel over the fireplace, that now sits on my mantel, that has been handed down from generation to generation for so long, ticked loudly in the silence. My mother said, "There." My father said nothing, just knocked his pipe bowl against the grey bricks of the fireplace; the ashes fell into the flames and were consumed. He opened the door and went out.

My mother disappeared into her bedroom and returned with her boar's hair brush. She sat in the chair my father had just vacated and motioned for me to kneel between her legs and lean back; my wings spread out under her thighs. She brushed my long lemon hair and the bristles dragging through it felt both stimulating and comforting. "Mama, did you do this?" I asked.

"Of course. Everyone does. Don't ask questions."

"Why?"

"Some things just are and we just do them, like eating and sleeping."

"Do you want me to go?"

"A mother must release her children, when it is time. Enough, now."

I wanted to ask, 'What's up there?' and 'What happened to Tomas?' but couldn't. Asking questions, particularly about the mountain, is not done. But I did manage one more: "What will happen to me up there?"

My mother got up and left the room.

When the clock struck ten, my father returned. I was naked before him, naked before both my parents, and I felt embarrassed, although now I realize that to them my budding womanhood was all but invisible and I was still very much their child. My father took the lantern from the nail on the wall, lit it and said, "Come, Renata."

"Bye, Momma," I called, but she turned away.

My father led me to the foot of the mountain at the cemetery, where the others were gathering with their parents. Ena, my best friend, born just hours before me, was there, and nine more.

"Johan is missing," someone noticed, and then someone else said, "There. He is coming."

That year there were twelve of us, the same number as our individual ages, the same as the hour when we must be sitting at the crossed roads.

We were directed to form a line and then ordered according to the month of our birth. It is not the way in our village to express emotions publically. Still, Johan's mother cried out— her son was first. As it happened, I was last. My father did not cry out, but his eyes looked haunted.

The line began moving as if of its own volition. Like lower life forms, we seemed to possess an instinct that directed us towards our goal.

The bare path through the trees was narrow—no adult could have passed without skin being shredded by the harsh briars—but still I wondered why the shrubs had not overgrown it. The thought crossed my mind: nothing can live here.

We climbed through the darkness in silence. The cold air chilled me through to my bones. The dirt was imbedded with pebbles that pierced the soles of my feet but, like the others, I was brave. It occurred to me how odd it was that no one ever went onto the mountain except this night once a year. I had never noticed animals on the mountain, and birds flew around it. I looked up. The full moon was just crossing the sky.

The climb took nearly an hour, leaving us time to spare. We found the crossroads easily and sat in a tight circle where the roads met, again by instinct. It was cooler here. A light snow was falling. We were so high that we had ascended through the clouds. Those same clouds, now below us, blocked the view of the valley. I could not see my home.

Ena and I sat side by side, our shoulders touching. There was shifting and coughing, but no one in the circle spoke—we had been warned not to. Ena and I smiled bravely at one another. Johan, being at the front end of the line, was on my other side.

The wind picked up. This new chill set my teeth to rattling. Why could we not build a fire? Hadn't midnight arrived? The moon looked very close. As I stared into that cool ancient face, something dark crossed it, making the moon scowl and my heart beat quickly.

I don't know who noticed first. All I remember was the shriek, and then turning, and staring as if transfixed at a sight I will forever see in my nightmares. All of us were frozen.

What landed on the ground nearby was huge and inhuman. With the moon as a backdrop, enormous wings spread, spanning six feet; I heard them rustle like crepe paper and watched them quiver. Long hair whipped behind the naked body; the face was in shadow. One of the children panicked and tried to bolt but was held back by another—the thing from the sky turned enough that I could see breasts, the nipples plump as if filled with milk for nursing.

Now I saw the face of this being. Flesh creased, withered really, and the thin lips split apart by fang-like teeth. I do not know if it was my imagination, but I saw no color in those eyes, just blank orbs that seemed to reflect everything. The silvery moonlight cast a glow that made this other-worldly being hideous but beautiful, and it could be because I saw her in this way, I was not so mesmerized as the others.

In a flash I understood why we were here, and what she needed. I also understood the implications of not sating that need. I knew I could not let any of my friend remain here, as Tomas had, sacrificing themselves.

"Go!" I told the others. "Hurry!"

Johan, last to arrive, was first to leave. Because he was the eldest, others followed immediately. Ena called to me, but I waived her on. And when I was alone with the monster, I turned to face her.

"Why do you drink only blood?" I asked boldly.

She stared at me a long moment, a bemused look on that decayed face, as if no one had asked her this before, or anything else. That face was bizarre, feral, yet possessed a beauty dark as death itself. She looked wild, untamed and untamable, like a all-powerful Fury, who answers to no one. And yet she answered me.

"You nourish me and I will nourish your people. Come." She beckoned with her long talons.

"Do you drink only once a year?"

Her eyes took on a fiery quality, like white heat. Still, she did not move towards me. "Once a year only. This is not so much to ask."

"You become young then?"

"Yes."

"And you drink all the blood, do you not?"

"Yes."

"Did you drink my brother's blood?"

"I do not know your brother. Each is the same to me. It grows late. Come."

"What does blood taste like?"

She was thoughtful for a moment. "Like waves of metallic fire. Like remembered sunlight. It tastes of life itself, refined."

"And are you alone the rest of the year?"

Here she paused. I sensed I had stepped over an invisible line. I felt my life hang in the balance.

But, as before, she answered me. "I am alone because I know no equal. Your people are children to me as you are a child to them."

Her blank eyes seemed to grow intense, as though a fire had been fanned behind them, and she looked ravenous.

Without knowing it at that time, I had stumbled on my own salvation, and my punishment. I questioned her all night, as the moon stood directly above the mountain top, as it descended the sky and the eastern horizon grew light. I do not know why she answered me, when I was not used to answers. But as the first light washed away the blackness, her features took on a dusty hue that made her seem old and faded, like a dried rose. At last she turned to go.

"Are you really our mother?" I asked. It would be my final question.

She turned back one last time. The light shining in those snowy orbs made them look hollow. "I am the giver of life and the bringer of death and I must be obeyed. You have brought my wrath upon the heads of your people and now they will feed me all the year."

She turned, hesitated, turned to look at me once more, then her wings flapped twice, creating chilling gusts of wind, and I struggled for balance. As she ascended, I realized in part what I had done and yet would not know until later the extent of it.

This year my eldest daughter, Elena, turned twelve. I make her wings, as my mother made mine, and her mother made hers. But unlike the women before me, I am not silent.

I tried to tell them, in the village, that if they do not question, nothing will alter. But they are afraid and declare that it is sacrilege to tamper with tradition. And many remember the winter twenty years ago. The plague that descended. The crops that would not yield. The madness that struck our village until the next All Hallow's Eve. Many blamed me, even though I asked them, "Is it fair that one should pay for all?" No one responded and yet I felt their condemnation when they did not come to the funeral of my mother and father.

"Elena," I assure my daughter, "we have had nineteen good and fruitful years in the village. Our harvests have been bountiful. Babies have been born healthy and our citizens have lived to old age and died in their beds. We can afford one lean and hard season."

I have told her the story, of how I saved my life, of why I believe I was spared, of the aftermath. She understands that, but there is more I need to tell her.

"But why do I have to go up there?" she asks.

"It is tradition," I say.

"But will she spare me because I ask her questions?"

I smile and tell her, "Someone must question her."

"But won't she punish us?"

I brush my daughter's long golden hair back. She closes her eyes and sighs. "She may again punish our people."

"Everybody will blame me, won't they?"

"In time, when enough have questioned, when perhaps your own daughter questions, our dark mother must see that her children have grown. She will not need to consume us to be filled. And we will no longer need to be consumed to gain her love. But come. It is time. Mother mountain waits."

Bats With Bite

The Shaft

———◦———

Celie could not bring herself to appreciate the air shaft. She didn't give a damn what happened tomorrow. Dust motes trapped in the concrete shaft could float back and forth forever in the sunlight, for all she cared. It was now, this minute, her first night in the apartment, that peering up her skylight at the slab of vertical tunnel overhead made her feel just how oppressive darkness could be. Until someone on a floor above switched on their bathroom light.

Pale yellow pierced the gloom immediately surrounding that window. It didn't effect the rest of the shaft nor last very long, still, it irritated her even more than the absence of light. Someone could be watching. She needed privacy.

She lighted three candles and turned off her bathroom light. The claw-footed tub nearly overflowed with rose-colored bubble bath. She hesitated then gingerly stepped in. Steaming water scorched her flesh and only mind over matter kept her from yanking her feet out. Instead, she bent, then sat and finally, sucking in air loudly through her teeth, submerged herself to the neck. I need this, she insisted, willing the pain away.

Above, another light flicked on. Annoyed, she glanced up. Second floor. The tenant she'd been informed was "old Mr. Morrison". She heard horking, then the toilet flush, the ordinary sounds human beings make. The light went out. He couldn't see her anyway. He was on the left side of the air shaft. Even if he opened his window the few inches the drop chains allowed, he wasn't at a good enough angle for the tub or toilet. Or her. And the candles helped.

But she wasn't worried. This first night of independence, out on her own in the world, filled Celie with excitement and nearly obliterated the paranoia her large and meddlesome family had instilled in her. She was the youngest of the backward brood and, she knew, the most impressionable. Maybe that was why a small worry gnawed away at her inside the way the hotter-than-hot water burned her skin. Hell, I can take care of myself, she thought stubbornly. She glared up the vertical tunnel. The blackness felt dense.

Celie coated one arm with suds and tried to concentrate on watching the iridescent pink bubbles pop, one by one. Moving in the hot water irritated her sensitive skin so she massaged the back of her neck slowly then rested her head against the plastic air cushion suctioned to the tub rim.

Tension drained. Eyelids fell. Pipes knocked.

Her eyes snapped open.

She hated this, when it was so late and she was half asleep and everything looked unnaturally bright. Stark. Suddenly she was angry with herself for not taking a modern apartment. She'd been so eager to put distance between herself and her intrusive relatives. Escape was more like it. And she'd had this idea, now, in retrospect naive and romantic, that old inner city buildings are charming, intimate and anonymous. Right, she thought. Rice paper walls, resident wildlife, the first flush toilets ever built. Who could ask for more?

She started to close her eyes again. They jerked open fast when the light went on. Top window. On the right.

That building was attached to the one she lived in like Siamese twins. The landlord told her it had been empty for months, waiting for repairs to be completed. Renovations were, as far as she knew, underway. Workmen would be hammering like maniacs in the morning, but who could be there this late?

She listened carefully. No water running. No usual bathroom noises. The light stayed on.

It was far up the shaft, crowded by decades of dust and gloom, so she couldn't see well but heard the window pop open. She had the feeling someone was watching.

The moment she thought that, the light went out. The angle's perfect, she realized, they can see me. Quickly she pulled an oversized bath towel from the rack and draped it across the tub. A sudden awareness hit hard—she was alone.

The silence was dense so when the light on the second floor to the right came on she jolted. Why am I not surprised, she thought. Like the one above, she heard the squeak and thud of the window opening. When the light went off, the blackness of the air shaft threatened to invade the room.

She waited, muscles tense. The bubbles had evaporated and the pink water cooled to an even more inhospitable temperature. Logic told her she was perfectly safe. No human being could fit through her skylight at the bottom of the tunnel. Besides, damn it, this was her bathroom, her apartment. She had her rights. She wouldn't be intimidated.

Whoever was in the building had moved down to the apartment next door; she could hear through the walls. As expected, the skylight next to her own lit up, casting a sick glow that stuck to the base of the air shaft.

Sounds of sliding glass. A shadow on the tunnel's grey wall. Movement above, then two eyes, laced with obsession. Barely human. Malevolent. Ancient as the darkness itself.

Celie grabbed the edge of the tub and, in one motion, vaulted up and out. Glass shattered. Sharp chunks and slivers gashed her shoulders. She screamed.

It soared through the opening, wings extended, and tackled her, already shape-shifting. His weight pressed her to the slippery floor tiles. She gasped, suffocating in a womb of chilled flesh.

His breath, the oppressive smell of him, came hot and stinking against her neck. Then two teeth, sharp and quick, pierced skin, muscle and artery. She cried out, "No!"

Struggling didn't help. She weakened.

Finally he sat up and flipped her onto her back.

"Bastard!" Celie screamed. His features were darkly attractive and generous like her own. Well-defined lips, smeared with her blood, split into an intolerably boyish grin. He offered her his wrist, teasing her, but she was in no mood for games. Celie tore into his flesh with vengeance, taking back what was rightfully hers.

"Ow! Don't be mad, Sis. Just missed ya, that's all."

Teaserama

The leggy beauty wearing impossibly high stilettos pranced across the silver screen. Tall, raven haired with bangs, midnight undergarments gracing her slim yet curvaceous pale figure, she seemed to be the only star of these unusual movies able to do anything more than hobble in the patent-leather shoes. She undulated with a frolicsome grace that ignited him, and his ashes had been long cold.

Much to his amazement, humanity was changing. Five centuries he had walked the earth, nightly supping from the veins of these crass mortals. What he had imbibed contained not just vital nourishment for him, but the sum total of his cretinous victims' values. He had come to see humans as less than insectoid, with nothing to offer him but the blood. But now, oddly, he felt an infusion of life where he had expected none.

Vlad rewound the film around the reel and re-played the short black and white story for the tenth time. *Varietease* was one of his favourites, featuring Lili St. Cyr, and, more to his taste, Miss Betty Page! This Betty was a marvel, the woman of his dreams, were he still able to dream. Fetching, attractive, and most of all playful in her sensuality. Females in his youth had expressed either violence towards him, or had proven passive enough to retain his interest. Early on, when natural life had bubbled hot in his veins, when he had been full of passion, a warlord, fighting the Turks to retain his territory, and his own countrymen for power, he demanded his women be subdued. Life had been brutal enough back then—his mortal death verified that fact. Why fight with a woman in the boudoir? Oddly, immortality proved far easier, not particularly violent, yet he found himself less than enthraled with the 'humanizing' global changes. He was alone. Always. Stalking vapid prey through the streets of European and North American urban forests, destined to find none in sympathy, no empathy from the living, none in the progressingly dispassionate centuries to inspire his appetites... This turn of the tide had left him depleted. Existence in a bland world produced ennui in one such as himself, one of immense substance. And he knew the cause: humanity. They were worse than peasants. Worse than the insects that crawled from the earth's graves. They viewed his state of ungrace far too simplistically, as they viewed their own pathetic lives. And that was the problem. They were neither terrified of him—hell bent on destroying him as those in the past had been—nor utterly enamoured. He lost interest in his sniveling soul-pale victims before he had drained the last drops of their vitae.

He watched the two lovelies cavort on screen, focusing mostly on Betty. She was young, winsome. She forced him to feel himself an anachronism, and that he could not, would not tolerate! He was Vlad Tepesh! Prince of Transylvania! King of the Living Dead! Lord of the Darkest Night! And he would have more than banality. He would have love.

As if out of a mist his celluloid vision turned towards the camera, towards him. He watched his pristine darling glide with the grace of a she-wolf. She played with the other, revelling in her role, whether as the giver or the receiver. Miss Page enjoyed herself to her naughty fullest. He longed for a woman who could enjoy herself. Who could appear so sweet and alluring and yet obviously kindle his intense passions. He deserved to enjoy himself as well. And, as always, he would have what he wanted.

The dark-haired beauty, who reminded him so much of his second wife, flirted with the camera lens. She seemed to stare right at him, a brazen, teasing look, one that he felt moved to tame. The other on screen punished her mildly—he would be more firm, that was certain. But even mild chastisement titillated him. This decade was truly a turning point in history, and like nothing else he had experienced. Oh, there had been French postcards, and those mild Victorian moving pictures at the turn of the last century. And he'd encountered a sufficient share of ladies of the night during his nocturnal wanderings. But never in several centuries had he witnessed such verve, such panache, such...full-blown erotic expression on a woman as fresh as the one he saw before him now.

Beside him lay an assortment of publications and film canisters, all featuring Miss Page: girlie magazines with cheesecake shots; *Cartoon and Model Parade No. 53*; various calendars; *Playboy Magazine*, January 1955, featuring Betty as the centrefold, photographed by Bunny Yeager...

Ah, Bunny Yeager. He remembered with pain spiking his heart the events of but one year ago. It had taken some time to find Betty, but when he did he acted at once. He discovered that Miss Page had gone to Florida, to be photographed by Yeager. Travel arrangements were made, and he arrived in Miami at the end of an arduous journey which spanned several days of riding by night on a train, only to discover after much searching that she had gone that day to a remote tourist attraction called Rural Africa, some seventy miles north of the city, and had not yet returned.

He discovered the location of her apartment—information in this less-congested city was not difficult to obtain with his powers—and there he awaited her return. She did return, but rather than retire, she proceeded to a main building. He watched her through a window, talking animatedly with several others, dining, relaxing, sewing a small leopard-skin garment out on the verandah while she chatted, one of the adorable outfits she wore. And all the while, his ardour grew. She was as effervescent in the flesh as on the screen. He determined that this night she would be his! Finally, just after 1:00 a.m., she left the main building for her cottage closeby. This was the first time he had found her alone. He watched her walk along the path, as stunned as a novice lover, unable to approach her, fearful of rejection. She entered her residence and bolted the door. He rebuked himself. How had he been reduced to this! He, a *vivode*, Prince of Wallachia! Destroyer of the Ottoman invaders, and the betrayers who called themselves countrymen! His childish hesitation now meant that she was inaccessible. He could not gain admittance without an invitation, and without contact with Miss Page, he would not receive one.

The frustration drove him to her window, in the alley at the back, where he peered inside through a break in the Venetian blinds. He watched her undress for bed. He held his breath; the sight of her sublime physique stunned him to silence. Such beauty felt unearthly, as if a cloud had parted and this angel had fallen from heaven—did they know she was missing? Unawares, his fingernails clawed the screen over the window. Only when she turned, a delicious look of terror streaking her features, did he realize what he had done.

Quick to remedy the situation, he decided that when she came to the window, he would instill the thought in her mind, through the glass, to open the window, to admit him. He pulled the screen away, for a better contact, and watched her snatch an article of clothing with which to cover herself and hurry toward him until she was so close he could only see her waist. He paused, waiting for the blind to lift.

"I'll give you two seconds to get away from this window or I'll blow your brains out!"

Startled by her booming voice, he had no idea she possessed a weapon. The pistol would not harm him, of course, but the noise would draw others. His sense returned, and he retreated, biding his time, until the following night, when he would find a way to meet her outdoors, to look into her eyes, to capture her will and make her his own.

But the following evening she was gone. Inquiries let him know that the photo shoot had been completed and Miss Page had returned to New York. He felt devastated. Thwarted like a mere schoolboy. Unable to grasp this failure. There had seemed nothing to do but return to New York himself, and plot out a further opportunity.

Varietease finished and the end of the film spun off the feeder reel. It was one of his favourites, but he liked the others as well, the ones with the girls play-spanking each other. The one where Miss Page helped tie another to an Oak. Miss Page was a woman of unusual thespian talents. She excelled as both the discipliner and the disciplined, and that he found exceptional. He especially enjoyed that odd contraption, so like a Medieval instrument of torture, on which a woman tied Miss Page, spread-eagled, upright, only to pull on both ends of the rope and lift the enchanting Betty off the ground. Four centuries of seduction of increasingly insipid mortals had left him a tad jaded; his libido had grown as quiet as had his once- beating heart. And now, at this juncture in history, in this metropolis of New York City, he was revived. Had he been capable of tears, he would have cried them— tears of joy.

A glance out the window and he could see how the night quivered. He felt youthful, driven by something other than pure bloodlust. This city was the hub of the universe. The dawn, as it were, of a proverbial new day. It also teemed with human beings. Finding blood was never a problem. Finding Miss Page alone had been. She was popular, always busy, always accompanied. Two years of effort on his part had resulted in constant frustration. But he sensed that time, though eternal, held an urgency he had not experienced for centuries, and he valued that tension.

He snapped off the projector and grabbed up his cane to begin the search for Miss Betty Page.

Irving Klaw's studios, he had only recently learned, lay close by, in a warehouse. Rumour had it, Klaw was shooting *Teaserama*, and Vlad hastened to make his way there before the filming was completed.

Enroute, he stopped at a kiosk to flip through a new publication, with still photos from *Strip-o-Rama*, one of her films. There was the sparkling Miss Page, in all her titillating glory! This era was indeed marvelous. Nothing left to the imagination. He felt he had finally come home in a sense, returning full-circle to the core of life. Finally society was opening, like the wounds of pierced flesh, and the lifeblood poured forth for all to drink at will. And at the centre, Miss Page, a woman into whom he seriously wanted to sink his fangs.

"She's a doll, alright. Have a gander at that, bub." The rat-like man who ran the kiosk nodded at a calendar hanging from the back wall.

Miss Page on a beach, in the sunshine—oh how she caused him to long for the sun!—wearing a sparse swimsuit. Smiling her engaging, teasing smile, her lithe body with the come-hither tilt of her hips...

"You buyin'?"

He turned toward the rat of a man. One glance at those rodent eyes and the creature was made nearly dumb, only murmuring, "Go ahead. Take it, mister."

Vlad threw the *Photoplay* volume at the vendor. He did not need these cheap imitations. By sunrise, he would possess the flesh and blood woman of his desires.

Klaw's studio lay hidden in the warehouse district, protected by meat packing plants and dry goods wholesalers. Vlad had been here before, many times, searching for Betty. But as dumb luck would have it, either she was elsewhere, or else accompanied by a gaggle of friends. Even when he'd staked out this premises nightly when they first began to shoot *Teaserama*, he could not find her alone. Tonight, though, he was determined. Tonight he would gain admittance to the building, then to the studio. And finally to Miss Page herself.

He waited until he saw someone head towards the entrance. No sooner had they entered the main door than he was behind, catching the door as it closed, calling out.

A young man delivering sandwiches from a delicatessen turned, a startled look denting his freckly face. It took no time for Vlad to imbed the proper words in his brain, and the youth soon repeated the magic phrase, "Sure, come on in."

Once inside, the warehouse was a maze of doors. Some sported signs: Friedman's Fruitcakes; The Button Hole; Crown Cork and Can... He wandered the twenty stories, disregarding the doors which obviously did not house a film studio on the other side, pressing his ear to the ones that gave little or no indication of what lay within. Finally, after much searching, he heard voices:

"Don't worry, honey, just gimme a big smile. It's gonna be alright." This accompanied by the sound of what might have been a crank.

It was do or die the true death. He knocked and heard a "Damn!"

The man who appeared at the crack the door opened was of ordinary height, with a dark moustache and intense, red-rimmed eyes. "Yeah?" he said suspiciously.

"I am searching for Betty Page."

"You and a two thousand other guys," he said. "What's your business with her?"

It took only seconds to mesmerize this man and to gain admittance.

Within lay a film studio in one large space, or what remained of it. The area was almost barren. Boxes had been packed and stacked near the door. Tripods were propped against the wall, and cameras and film canisters had been gathered together. A woman in midlife, the only other person in the room, wanted to know, "Irving, who's this guy?"

The man named Irving shook his head, as if waking from sleep.

"You a fed?" she asked.

"Nah. He don't look the type," Irving said.

"I am searching for Miss Page. Where may I find her?" Vlad said.

"That's anybody's guess. She took off last week, like all the others, God knows where. Just after they started in on us."

"Make yourself clear!" Vlad demanded, impatience rising alongside the fear gnawing up his spine.

"The House of Representatives. You know, the federal government? Don't you read the papers?"

The woman moved closer. "The House Unamerican Activities Committee. They figure we film smut and that ain't exactly American or something."

"Meaning?" Vlad asked, but after five centuries walking the earth, he already understood.

"Meaning," the man said, "they shut us down. That there's all that's left. A copy."

Vlad walked to the canister the man pointed at and picked it up. *Teaserama* the label read. All that remained of Betty Page.

"Hey! You can't take that!" the man shouted, as Vlad turned towards the door, cradling the canister against his stone-cold heart.

One look from the Prince of Darkness, a look not intended to mesmerize, a look that conveyed a depth of pain no mortal could bear to see for long, caused Irving Klaw to say softly—and Vlad knew it was not out of terror but out of empathy—"I got the original anyways, or Friedman does. Take it. You need her."

And he did.

Virtual Unreality

"Damned loathsome era!" Randolph muttered as he passed through the intricate grating at the door of his family tomb.

He surveyed the cemetery with growing disgust. The cretins had been at their dirty work again. Unearthing ancient bones. Toppling tombstones. Relocating antique marble crypts. Devouring the placid landscape to erect yet another ghastly concrete rectangle to assault the sky. Whatever happened to rest in peace? Hadn't his estate paid for care *in perpetuum*? Randolph could barely recall the last time he'd seen a newly dug grave in this burial yard. The current fad for cremation was frightening, and it appeared to be getting out of hand.

He stalked the necropolis path toward the electronically secured main gates. It was late, *le soleil* had long ago set but the street lights ahead were brilliant as the sun at noon.

Damned if this vampire isn't famished, he thought, passing like a mist through the wrought iron. As an afterthought, he realized his instinct to begin earlier had been right on the money. Supper was not as easily procured as it once had been. Although his designated dining domain had become crammed with reeking humanity, it was difficult to find a lone mortal and nigh on impossible to get one alone. Who invited in strangers nowadays?

Speeding vehicles clogged the main street, vomiting exhaust fumes and shinning bright headlights in his face. He squinted. At least he had the satisfaction of not having to breathe in this wretched pollution. It didn't take a physician, even though he had practiced as one for the 40-odd-years of his temporal existence, to figure things out. The lungs, as any fool should know, pass poisons into the blood stream. These millennium crashers as a whole were duller than any generation he'd encountered in the last two hundred years. It wasn't enough for them to corrupt their bodies with foul air and water and countless toxins along their food chain, but they had to resort to illicit pharmaceuticals and carnal practices that spread deadly diseases. Blood, in general, had become so impure even he could barely stomach it. He'd had a number of close calls. Just last week he'd had a *tête-à-tête* with a maiden who, unbeknownst to him, suffered Twentieth Century Disease. The remainder of that week had been spent sneezing uncontrollably. Experiences like that one and worse had forced him on several occasions to degrade himself and pilfer from a blood depository, where at least the chilly fluid of life had been screened.

He reached the corner of Barton and Wells Streets, the fatal intersection where he had been sucked dry a couple of centuries before. It was inopportune that he had died at a crossroad, not to mention being the seventh son of a seventh son. If only his dolt of an heir had had the sense not to inter him at yet another crossroad, and during a full moon to boot, his vampiric condition might have been nullified and he might not be here now, struggling with this asinine global village. But, of course, they'd wasted his hard-earned money and built no less than a mausoleum in which to store his bloodless remains. Well, damned if he hadn't wreaked revenge! He'd shown them. Or had he? After all, they'd gone on to their heavenly reward while he was trapped here, in this godforsaken nest of techno imbeciles who'd managed to convince themselves that nothing significant had occurred prior to their birth.

His dark musings were cut short by a short-haired blonde in her early twenties who stopped short next to him at the curb. She wore silver tights and a skin-clinging black skirt, so short it would have been considered indecent as an undergarment in his day. At least a head and a half taller than Randolph, she glared down at him—no doubt feigning boredom—and tapped the toe of her cowboy boot, impatient for the blood-red traffic light to change.

Although he wore formal clothing and a full opera cape, she, as was the case with many of her contemporaries, did not appear to find that peculiar. Even a hundred years ago his attire would have had this sweet damsel swooning in his arms, one of the few perks, as they would now call them, of his condition. Today's fashion reflected the mental state of its lunatic wearers. Oddly enough, he actually blended with the throngs of bizarrely-dressed urbanites.

The blonde strode out onto the asphalt. Her slim thighs interested him, as did her swaying backside. In more civilized times females had acted demurely; they had been ladies. Perhaps the early twenty-first century wasn't all bad.

With midnight fast approaching, he decided to follow her along Barton going West. The sidewalk was crowded and he was jostled repeatedly. Finally, he hissed at a group of ruffians with wires hanging out their ears who had forced him onto the road. One young fellow with purple hair dangerously spiking outward a good two feet from his scalp and wearing an Edwardian crushed velvet jacket, crinkled up his pimply face and snarled, "Halloween's next month!" His cohorts laughed.

Randolph entertained thoughts of disconnecting the holligan's head from his torse and finding new orifices for those wires, but there were far too many witnesses. Besides, he wanted to intercept the blonde. He sighed. The night might indeed be young, he thought, but I, alas, am much older.

The girl hailed a taxi at the next corner and Randolph did likewise. "Kindly follow that cab," he instructed the driver, a young Rastafarian, who glanced at him in the rearview mirror, saw nothing, adjusted the mirror and finally looked over his shoulder.

"My man, you don't be no *Candid Camera?*"

"My good fellow, she's escaping!" Randolph said, waiving a hand of dismissal at this lackey.

The driver faced front, checked his mirror again, shook his head, and stepped on the gas.

The blonde disembarked on Devereaux Street. As his taxi pulled up behind the one driving away, Randolph watched her press the doobell of a non-descript townhouse.

Randolph mesmerized the driver sufficiently to cause him to forgo the fare. The girl had been admitted into the residence and he hurried behind her. His fingers curled around the door frame just before the door shut. He nudged the door open and peered inside. A steep flight of stairs led up to what must have been the upper apartment. Sharp-edged music blasted down to the street level when a door above opened briefly. As he went up the stairs, a couple, apparently intoxicated, wobbled down. Half-way, they encountered Randolph.

"Hot!" the girl said, grabbing the hem of Randolph's cape as she passed so that it billowed behind him. "Get one!" she ordered her mate, a tall, pallid lad who, by way of response, grunted.

The door to the flat stood ajar, but Randolph was powerless to enter a private domicile *sans invitation*. Intellectually, he never could comprehend this invisible barrier, but physically felt it the way he had once experienced the weight of air pressure on his body when the moisture level increased. He waited until a young man smoking a very slim cigarette came within earshot.

"Excuse me," Randolph said.

The fellow stopped and turned in his direction.

"If I'm not mistaken, this is a gala."

"You've got total recall."

"How may an invitation be secured?"

"Blaze on in."

Randolph entered.

The room was large and had it been empty of humans the sparse furnishings would have been more obvious. Two minimalist sofas; several bizarrely twisted metallic lamps. Stainless steel shelving had been nailed to almost every wall. The shelves held a dozen television sets, each tuned to a different station, plus a clutter of *de rigueur* home entertainment units and other electrical objects.

Milling mortals, in all their effluvia, crammed the space. Air waves littered with a cacophony they defined as music entertained these dulllards. The air itself carried a haze of burning tobacco and other plants. At least the track lighting was dimmer than street lights. Randolph sneered. Palaces of conceit! These creatures were so vain. They couldn't pass any of the dozens of mirrors without preening. He had never acted in such a narcissistic fashion even when he had been able to view his rather handsome *visage* in refective glass.

He wandered the periphery, a soldier stalking the enemy camp, searching out his prey. He had just spotted her, entering a darkened room, when someone breathed garlic into his face, making him cringe.

"Got a light?"

Composure recovered, he glanced down at a girl plump as a peasant, wearing a red taffeta gown that revealed an amazing amount of *décolleté*. She wiggled a slim black-papered cigarette in his face and grinned suggestively. Her upper front teeth were streaked with the crimson lip paint so in vogue.

"I do not smoke," he bowed deeply, "cigarettes."

"Yeah, hardly anybody does."

One sniff of the acrid air convinced him she was deluding herself. The nubile girl rocked her ample hips in one direction and her bouncing bosom in another in time with the staccato drum beat. She lifted a bottle of ale to her lips and drank long and deep. Randolph sighed. When had grace and charm succumbed to the vulgar and banal? Subtle aesthetics went wanting here. Even his chesty companion pursing her carmine lips could not hold his attention. The atmosphere was so draining that he briefly entertained the idea of giving up the chase altogether.

But it occurred to him that he had gone to bed hungry on one too many sunrises, and that grated. Damned if these vile creatures of daylight would best him again!

Available as this immediate morsel might be, he could not bring himself to imbibe from one so coarse when a shade more refinement was but half a room away. Besides, the reek of that odoriferous root-from-hell on her breath dampened his desire.

Out of the corner of his eye he spotted the blonde peeking out the door briefly before heading back inside. Whatever else was going on in that room, she was there. His potential victim. His *amour de la nuit*. The wanting of her made her that much more appealing.

I am vampire! he thought proudly, puffing out his chest and gripping the edges of his cape in a dramatic fashion. She will succumb.

"Ever done VR?" the fleshy girl asked.

He looked blankly at her.

"Virtual Reality. I saw you checking out the door. Wanna try? Your mind'll go ballistic."

"An excellent proposal, my dear." He offered his guide an arm.

The room was lightless, but his vision, like a cat's, utilized the stray rays seeping under the door and he was able to see clearly enough.

His intended slouched demurely on the only piece of furniture in the room, a metal trunk. Chewing on a cuticle. Waiting. In the middle of the room two youths wearing large, outlandish gloves and bulky helmets that covered their eyes moved in a slow-motion dance, bodies twisitng and jerking to a peculiar rhythm. He watched for a few moments, wondering what they were doing.

"Dibs on *Mondo Midnight*," the fatty tidbit by his side squawked.

He looked down at her, knowing his glowing orbs would capture her attention. He was not mistaken.

The girl's eyes widened and the pupils contracted rapidly before they expanded. He sent a very strong suggestion her way and within moments she left the room.

Randolph strode purposefully toward the blond. Surely she heard or felt him near? But, in fact, she barely exhibited signs of life. One sniff advised him that she had managed, within the time it takes to hammer a stake into a heart swollen with black blood, to send powerful chemicals pounding through her own heart. This would not do. She raised her glass to her lips and he carefully removed it from her grasp.

She turned her head in his direction. Her pupils did not seem to have the strength to alter from their dilated state. She did not look startled nor did she seem annoyed or pleased. He thought of mesmerizing her but the effect would be wasted. Abstinence from further intoicants and time would work far better.

The two young men began removing their gear. The equipment, all wired together, was plugged into an outlet, no doubt to recharge. They each raised an arm and slapped hands together. One said, "All right!" in a self-satisfied tone and the other simply replied, "Cool", that accursed non-sequitur of the twentieth century, of late divided into two distinct syllables.

The moment they departed, Randolph locked the door. He sat alone with his lovely lady, pulling her head onto his shoulder, stroking her spiky golden locks, heroically restraining his lustful urges until a sufficient cleansing of her system had taken place. He imagined a couple of hours would do. After all, this was his one meal of the evening; he intended to enjoy it.

However, the waiting grew boring and to entertain himself, Randolph decided to investigate the technical costumes. Electricity was the bane of his existence. It created daylight glare at inappropriate hours, and exposed him to video cameras which refused to record his image. Despite being revolted by this hellish invention of electricity, he recognized that for his own protection he must keep abreast of the latest developments.

He left his damsel fair reclining against a potted palm and slipped the helmet over his head and the awkward gloves onto his hands. The room went black. A sudden vulnerability almost overcame him until he reminded himself that he was, in fact, nearly indestructible.

Randolph had seen the two young men pressing buttons on the gloves and he too pressed a button. His field of vision became illuminated, the color of a full moonlit night. Randolph was delighted to find himself in a cemetery.

He strode along the crystalline path, and promptly slammed into a solid, yet invisible object. Feeling through the gloves proved impossible so he removed one and lifted the helmet. He'd walked into a wall! Sheepishly, he glared at his bride of the night. She was oblivious.

Randolph recalled that the two youths had moved slowly, sliding, relying on the handset to guide them. He quickly discovered that by pointing, his body would move automatically to where he wanted it to go.

Passing sculpted marble effigies sparkling in the moon's glow, he took himself farther into the nocturnal paradise. This, he thought, is more like it. The relaxed atmosphere of the necropolis was one in which he felt at home.

Up ahead lay a marble crypt, similar to his own, but far more elaborate. He stopped to read the inscription:

Countess Elizabeth Bathory
1560-1614

Now this was interesting. He ran his hand along the smooth, cool stone, wondering if it had been imported from Italy, as had the stone of his mausoleum. If so, her heirs had paid a pretty penny. He was so preoccupied with these thoughts that he almost missed the pale form darting across the graveyard.

"Hello!" he called. When there was no response, he pointed in the general direction in which she had gone. Beyond a gnarled sycamore he found her huddled on a stone bench, face in hands, weeping uncontrollably. At his approach, she looked up. A vision of gossamer and lace, her diaphanous gown gleamed nearly as white as her alabaster skin. Hair black as Poe's raven twined in curls down her ivory shoulders. Her eyes were huge and dark, breath-taking, had he the breath to take away. From those almond pools, large tears dropped and ran in rivulets down her cheeks to the corners of lush crimson lips. Randolph was moved.

He sat beside her and slid an arm of comfort around her shoulders. Her small head fell onto his chest. He stroked her coal tresses as her body heaved and sobbed. "There there, my dear. What could be so terrible?" Even as he spoke the words, his eyes focused on her slender throat and the vein he knew awaited just beneath the surface.

She moved her face so that she looked up into his. So soft and vulnerable. A woman of refinement, of breeding. One of his own class, no doubt. A true damsel in distress. Her blood called to him.

He brushed the silken hairs back from her shoulder to better expose that tender area. Suddenly, her brown eyes blackened and a snakelike tongue darted fiercely out of her mouth. Two incisors rivaling his own snapped forward at an astonishing speed and clamped onto his neck.

He shoved her away from him. Her features turned feral. Her full lips were stained ruby. Instinctively, a trace memory of a night centuries ago forced his hand to his throat. It came away streaked with blood. But how could that be? He had not imbibed tonight. This vixen-from-hell could not have drawn anything from him.

She lunged. They struggled. Randolph was strong but she was his equal. In fact, the harder he fought her, the more her strength increased. Preposterous! he told himself. Fear for his unnatural life welled within him.

The battle seemed endless, neither one gaining. As his strength ebbed, so hers seemed to fail as well. He could not get away, he could not dominate her.

Suddenly, brilliant sunlight flodded the cemetery. Randolph screamed. His body jerked backward and he toppled. Panic seized him.

Invisible demon hands grabbed him and he fought them. A pounding reverberated through his head. Perhaps it's the Door to Hell, he thought, and cried, "Am I dead at last? Is this the end?"

All at once a weight was lifted from his skull. Randolph stared into the face of a werewolf. No, a shaggy-haired youth with bad teeth.

"You're hogging the equipment, man. Piss off!"

The gloves were pulled roughly from his hands, the wires unwound from his body. Randolph struggled to get a grip on what had happened. He felt his throat again. His hand came away dry.

The blonde he had stalked this night had vanished. As he staggered outdoors in confusion, he realized to his dismay that the sky was lightening. How could so much time have passed? He had less than an hour to find shelter.

There were no taxis to be had and despite his weakness from lack of feeding, and the fear of being spotted, he altered form on the sidewalk and flew back to the graveyard. If his heart were still functioning, it would be pounding.

Work crews had begun arriving for another day of demolishing the past. Carefully, he skittered from ancient tree to crumbling tombstone, dodging the burning rays that cut the horizon. Randolph flung his arms upward to protect his face and head and was rewarded with seared flesh.

He regained the safety of his tomb, skin still smoking. Hunger seized him and his body cramped. He stumbled into his sarcophagus, trembling.

As he yanked his coffin lid closed, he wondered about this era, when the electronic dead were more frightening than real demons. And more effective. Perhaps his time had come and gone. He had outlived his usefulness as a dark and dangerous force. Progress had buried him.

On the other hand, that vampiress was charming in her way. And cunning, a skill he admired. He could picture her now, a cameo of loveliness, not like these razor-edged modern temptresses.

An image of his delectable Elizabeth lodged in his brain. Ah, to sleep perchance to dream of her—if only he could dream! And then there was the virtual daylight. He had not wallowed in daylight for centuries.

The noise of the bulldozers should have kept him awake, but he felt calm and peaceful, and inexplicably hopeful. Randolph fell into a somnambulant state making plans for the future. He hoped the new crypt site would have electricity.

The
Unquiet Undead

Farm Wife

—◦—

Noma stationed herself at the back porch and propped the screen door open with her left foot. The sun hadn't set but one hour ago and already the Napanee sky was the color of ashes from the woodburner. Out past the pale tripod fencing and across the dying rye fields she saw Bert shuffling, Dog by his side. The sickness drained him. And left him hungry. Hungry all the time. Lord knows she fed that man a baker's dozen meals a day, but it was never enough. The more he ate, the thinner he got. Wasted. Just this morning she noticed he barely cast a shadow.

A mosquito trying to sneak into the house paused on her meaty upper arm. Yard was swanning with the last of 'em. She watched the bloodsucker poke its snout into a pore. "Want blood you'll get blood," she promised. Her skin began to itch bad but she made herself wait. Easy now. Ball the fist and knot the shoulder like her daddy had showed her. Noma's work-developed muscles tensed. She believed she could feel the strong blood forced up that chute.

The sucker went rigid.

Swelled to triple size.

Probably didn't even think about getting away.

She flicked the bloody corpse into the coming night and scratched her wound.

Noma shut the screen door but continued watching Bert make his way slowly toward the house. Sure is a stubborn man, she thought. Had been the forty-odd years she'd known him. Her daddy'd warned her, said it ran in Bert 's family, but she wouldn't listen. When Bert first come down with the sickness, she tried getting him over to the hospital. But he didn't trust city-trained doctors, didn't trust doctors at all, especially since his sister. Noma couldn't blame him, though. Seeing Ruby lying like milkweed fluff on those crisp sheets, color of white flour and brittle as dead leaves, eyes shot with blood and sunk back into her head, breath rank, gums shrunk up from the teeth like that... God, what a waste.

The doctors claimed it was some fancy kind of anemia. Gave her stuff but it didn't make the slightest bit of difference that Noma could see. Bert did the right thing in bringing her home. Ruby stayed upstairs in the room next to them, fading day by day, withering to less than nothings, just like Bert was now, until one morning when Noma took up eggs and bacon and found that Ruby had departed. "Best that way," Bert said. Noma had to agree.

And now it's him, she thought. As he reached the vegetable garden, even in the poor light she could see his bones pressuring the skin to set them free. His face wasn't more than a skull, with hardly any flesh for that pale hide to stretch across, and just a tuft of red on top. He lifted an arm and waved—she knew how hard that was for him.

As Bert reached the porch, Noma stepped out, ready to give him a hand up the steps, but he shrugged her off. You old curmudgeon, she thought. Even now, when he can use it most, he won't take no help. Well, that's just like a farmer, isn't it?

By the time she'd latched the screen door and closed and locked the inside one, he was at the refrigerator, dragging out the apple pie she'd baked this afternoon. He got a dessert plate from the cupboard and placed a hearty slice of pie on it. That slice went right back into the refrigerator. Out came the cheddar, and pure cream she'd whipped. He plunked himself down in front of the bulk of the pie, helped himself to a wedge of cheese the size of Idaho and scooped seven or eight kitchen spoons of milk fat onto the whole mess. She figured by eating so much, he fooled himself he wasn't sick.

"Cuppa coffee?" she asked.

He grunted and nodded but didn't pause.

Noma plugged in the kettle, but before the water got a chance to boil the pie tin was empty and he was back for that abandoned slice.

She measured freeze-dried coffee into two mugs—one twice the size of the other—and glanced out the window while she poured water over it. Gonna be cool tonight—October tended to be like that. Leaves on the willow been gone over a week; branches swayed in the breeze like a woman's hair. Might be a harvest moon come up, if the sky stayed clear. Low on the horizon. And full. She checked the calendar. Nope. Full moon tomorrow night. Be plenty to do come sunrise.

When Bert finished the pie be leaned his skinny self back in the chair and belched loud, then patted his stomach, or what used to be a stomach but had become so bloated he looked like he swallowed a whole watermelon. "Waste not want not," he said, and she agreed. She handed him his coffee and he took it to the living room. She heard the television; sounded like a sports show.

About eleven Noma put Dog out and they went upstairs. Bert tossed and turned, keeping her awake for a time, but she must have dozed off because she woke when she heard the stairs creak as he stumbled down. The refrigerator door opened and closed. Opened and closed again. Then the back door. She screen door slammed. She turned onto her side and pulled the feather pillow over her ear and went back to sleep.

Noma got up with the sun. Down in the kitchen she cleared the mess Bert had left. She opened the back door to let Dog in and fed him the scraps. The sky was packed with clouds the color of cow's brains, the air snappy. *Farmer's Almanac* promised frost tonight.

When breakfast was out of the way and she'd fed the chickens and pigs and milked the cows and turned them out to pasture, Noma harvested as much of the Swiss chard from the garden as she could—two and a half bushel baskets worth. She washed and blanched the iron-rich greens then stuffed them in airtight plastic bags that she sealed for the freezer. Bert hated chard, hated vegetables on principle, he said, but Noma couldn't get enough.

There was bed making, washing to do, some mending, lunch to get ready and eat, vacuuming, and a call to the feed store to see if that new corn and soya mix for the pigs was in yet. It wasn't.

Around four Noma began supper. Hadn't seen Bert all day. Didn't expect to. Still, she cooked up a mess of chard, and a ton of beef stew, the way she'd made a big lunch and breakfast, just in case.

Around six the cows came back. She locked them up in the barn and on her way to the house looked across the rye. The fields had faded to the color of dry bone. No sign of Bert. Not surprising. Still.

Noma watched reruns of that show with the fat woman but it wasn't very funny this week. She crawled into bed early, not quite ten-thirty. She'd done all she could, all anybody could, but sleep wasn't about to help her out tonight.

The eaves creaked. The wind picked up and howled the way it can. The house her daddy left her was old but solid. Noma grew up here, married here, had her kids, buried her folks. Through every season, lean and plenty—she was used to the sounds.

But when Dog howled at the moon, well...Bert always looked after Dog. She went to the window at the back and was about to warn the mutt to settle himself or else but stopped. Dog wasn't making a peep now. He stood quivering, scruffy tail between his legs, ears back, about to bolt. And staring at Bert.

A cloud lifted from the bloated moon and Bert turned his face up. The sickness was all over him. Eyes flecked with red like the blood that spurts from a leghorn when you chop the head off. He'd turned into a skeleton and what flesh he had left the moon showed was a kind of whitewashed blue. "Noma," was all he said. He grinned at her and she saw his gums had receded; his teeth reminded her of the sharp teeth on the combine. But the worst of all was his shadow. It was gone.

"Ain't letting you in," she told him firmly.

His eyes got hard and fiery red like sumach fruit. He stepped up onto the porch, out of her sight. She heard him rattling the back door. "Noma," he called again, so pathetic it got to her.

Despite her better judgment, she went down to the kitchen and opened just the inside, keeping the screen door between them.

"Best you be off," she told him. He cocked his head to one side—that always softened her up. The yellow kitchen light gave him some color. "Noma," he whispered, like they were in bed together.

She shook her head but opened the screen door.

He was on her in a second, pitchfork teeth tearing into her throat. Noma'd always been a big strong woman, but he was stronger—she'd discovered that early in their marriage. This was more so. He stank like the compost heap and his skin rivaled the frosty air. It was plain enough, he was starving, she was supper.

He held her against the kitchen table. She felt the iron-blood being drawn from her like milk from a cow. Wasn't but one thing to be done, what her daddy had taught her.

Noma worked slow, tensing the muscles up from her legs, through her privates and stomach, her arms, chest and back. When that was done, she eased up a second. One final overall squeeze did the trick.

Bert looked like he'd been slammed by a bale of hay. Blood gushed from his mouth, nose, and ears. His eyes popped wide. He swelled fast, the way the skin does when you're frying up chicken. A funny sound, kind of a cross between her name and a goose hissing, started to rise out of him but didn't get much of a chance.

Noma shook for a while but figured there wasn't much point to that. The clock over the stove read two-thirty. She glanced out the window. Frost had taken the last of the chard. The waste of it troubled her.

The walls and ceiling were splattered, the floor slime. She cleaned up what she could of the gory mess, then opened the door. Dog bounded in, happy to gobble the scraps.

Noma dabbed alcohol on her neck and checked the clock again. Time to get herself to bed. Sunrise wasn't far off. Tomorrow there'd be plenty to do. Always is for a farm wife.

Root Cellar

As Vadim struggled to get out of the Toyota, rain slammed him back. Nearby maple branches, bereft of leaves, clung to one another. The mid-winter sky was dead-gray but he noticed black storm clouds rush to squelch even that little light.

Five strides and Vadim hit the porch of the farmhouse, just as thunder broke. Lightning cracked a willow across the road, severing a branch. *An omen*, he thought, shivering, hating himself for even thinking that way. The way she had taught him to think. He hurried indoors.

The 'new' part of his grandmother's house, built seventy- five years ago, looked the same. Too-tall ceilings. Cavernous rooms. Sparsely-patterned wallpaper. Under the dust covers, like stern guardians, lay furniture Vadim had no intention of exposing. His memories were olfactory and reeked of blood and decay. He would not be here now if Lola had not gone out of the country. Lola, his younger sister, was still a baby at twenty. Lola desperately pleaded for specific memorabilia before he boarded up the property forever.

Vadim had no such desires. His memories of years spent in this house were of dead space, the weighted stillness as heavy as his grandmother's hand. He had distanced himself mentally and eventually physically from her insidiousness. And soon the disconnection would be permanent.

He glanced into the kitchen. The electricity had been shut off three months ago, but lightning flashed; it was frightening how nothing had changed. Except the corner. No willow switch stood ready for duty. Still, he would not have been surprised to see his grandmother's severe face in the doorway or hear her diseased rantings echo through the rooms.

Vadim went to the cupboard above and to the left of the sink. Second shelf at the back. He retrieved the empty sugar bowl with the butterfly on the lid that Lola wanted. He felt no sentimental feelings, just a sense of claustrophobia, as if the past were crushed against the present, intent on devouring the boundaries, desperate to consume it. He hurried upstairs.

The master bedroom his grandparents had shared sixteen years ago when Grandpa Bentz died was as silent as ever. The lifeless blue duvet had been flung across the foot of the bed. His grandmother ended her existence wrapped in that comforter, alone in a pool of foul-smelling excrement. Alone until her rotting flesh had been discovered. "Death only comforts the living," she had said with authority often enough. The clock in the corner no longer ticked and he was grateful.

He crossed the short hallway and took the attic stairs to the cramped and airless rooms to which he and Lola had once been banished. In his: wall cracks, as familiar and permanent as the creases of disapproval in his grandmother's face. A small dresser, its mirror wavy with age, unable to offer a true reflection. Vadim's single bed—springs that creaked so easily he had been afraid to breathe. That had creaked too often in rhythm to willow switches imprinting the fanily's ancient beliefs beyond his bare skin and deep into his cells.

In Lola's room he found the glass unicorn music box and carried it and the sugar bowl down the narrower rear stairs leading to the old part. He entered a shabby room that dated back two hundred years. Back to the fierce great-great-grandparents whom he had heard so much about. The ancestors who had immigrated from the old country where they had been persecuted. He had never felt safe in this part of the house.

Vadim paused. Outside black clouds smothered all light. He trembled as he reached into his raincoat pocket to pull out the flashlight. The sugar bowl slipped from his fingers. It hit the sloped hardwood and, even before he dropped the beam onto the pieces, Vadim knew it had shattered. Fear gripped him, the old, suffocating terror. But no ghost bent on punishment materialized. He exhaled; his nerves were on edge.

A flicker of blue lightning showed him something peculiar and

Vadim ran the flashlight beam over sills of the three large windows. "Mother of..." he whispered. Each sill was littered with fly carcasses, an inch thick. And the floor below the windows. And by the door. Thousands. No, tens of thousands. Black and iridescent green. Crisp hollowed shells that crunched beneath his soles. They clustered near the routes of egress but for them there had been no escape from this place.

Vadim no longer worried about the sugar bowl, he just wanted out before this tomb-of-the-dead sealed him in. But Lola had only asked for one thing more. Another object to cement her fantasy of happy memories and relegate the reality to insubstantial phantoms. The two of them were all that was left now. He needed her to ground him in the present, a world cleansed of superstition. *Take it easy*, he thought. *Grandma Bentz is gone. I'll be out of here in five minutes.*

The door to the root cellar was locked, as it always had been, but he broke the rusted padlock easily. The hinges squeaked as the door, warped from age and the moisture imbedded in this part of the house, scraped the floor.

Moldy air wafted out. Vadim aimed his light like a weapon into the appalling darkness. Ashamed, he watched his hand shake and heard ragged breath.

I can't do it, he thought. Memories of nights spent in the root cellar, crouched beneath the stairs, the smell of earth and vegetation and rot clogging his nostrils. And the sounds. Like nothing he had heard since, except in dreams. Over time he had learned to hum softly, loud enough to cover the noise, low enough not to bring down Grandma Bentz.

The doll Lola needed had been buried in a storage trunk for a decade and a half. The trunk in the cellar. Now that he'd broken the sugar bowl, there was no way to avoid getting it.

He stepped down into the dark pit. Cobwebs attacked his face and he gasped. "Weakling!" he admonished, repeating the word hurled so often at him. A word that must have traveled through generations.

Along the left of the stairs was a wall of shelves stocked with pickles and preserves. He read the aging labels from the lowest shelf up: chili sauce; corn relish; pickled cauliflower; carrots and dills dating back to 1790. A jar of murky contents, the yellowed label smudged. Beets, maybe. These had been here when he as a child, since before his grandmother was a girl. Every generation added to the store and Grandma

Bentz contributed the row second from the top. She had not allowed any of the jars to be touched, calling them, "Memories." Food uneaten. Life preserved forever.

The steps creaked in familiar spots as Vadim made his way to the dirt floor. He waved the light into each corner. The steamer trunk sat furthest from the stairs. In front of the metal door.

He placed the unicorn securely in his coat pocket and tucked the flashlight under one arm, ready to tackle this lock. But the latch was open, as if someone had expected him to come this way. Vadim glanced at the door and listened. Nothing.

He lifted the lid of the trunk. On the left, as if unaware of her surroundings, Lola's porcelain doll grinned up at him.

Only two other objects competed for his attention. A piece of barn board with post cards nailed to it. A small black coffin.

At the sight of the coffin, Vadim shook with fear and rage. Tears threatened to swell over his eyelids and he could not stop himself from yelling "Bitch!" She knew him so well. She had tricked him. Again.

He was startled by a noise behind the door. A rat. Or his imagination. He did not believe either.

Vadim wanted to grab the doll and bolt but decades of anger solidified. And he was curious. He lifted the board and ran the light from left to right along both rows. Each Victorian card was a pastel sketch. Together the eight pictures told a story:

WOMAN ALONE, HAPPILY SWINGING ON PORCH SWING.
MAN IN CLOAK APPROACHES.
MAN KISSES WOMAN ON NECK.
WOMAN DEAD IN COFFIN.
WOMAN RISES TO JOIN MAN.
MAN AND WOMAN KISS BOY ON NECKED
BOY DEAD IN COFFIN.
BOY RISES TO JOIN WOMAN AND MAN

A quaint Gothic record of family madness, he thought. *To be handed down from generation to generation with the silver.* But he had no intention of passing it further.

Vadim placed the board carefully back into the trunk. He snatched up the doll and stuffed it in his other pocket, ready to abandon this prison forever. Yet he felt compelled to look inside the coffin. She must have known he would. "You'll die of curiosity," Grandma Bentz had always predicted. He had believed she intended to fulfill that prophesy.

He picked up the crude wooden box and shook it but had no sense of what lay within. Less than a foot long, three inches at the widest part, shaped like an old-fashioned casket. A morbid miniature in flat black. The dead crawled from his memory: A nighthawk he had buried in a box he made, much like this one. His mother and father, killed in a barn fire. Grandpa Bentz who knows how he died. It was only his grandmother's corpse he had not viewed. Neither he nor Lola attended the service. Nor went to the cemetery. "If you don't witness the dead, how do you know they are?" Grandma Bentz had repeated at every demise, and the words haunted him now.

Vadim used his car key to pry between the lid and the box. The birch was hard and he was careful to wedge the metal in and lift the nails without damaging the wood. Images formed in his mind, gruesome pictures, parts severed from the living, stolen away from the light, drained of vitality, suspended in darkness forever to shrivel and emaciate slowly.

The lid was a quarter inch above the box and he was sweating. Suddenly time and space expanded. Endless. Hopeless. The eternity he had always feared clawed at the edges of his consciousness.

There was no point in hesitating and Vadim no longer considered it. Instead he struggled to defend himself from his most recent ancestor's bequest. A gift that he would leave to rot in the belly of this house. That would end with him and Lola, the last of a tortured line.

He yanked the lid away. The root cellar became a frozen grave. "What did you expect?" he chided, his voice unfamiliar and cold in the hollowness.

A sharp wooden stake lay inside the casket. Who had she intended it for? She had forced him to this point just as she had meticulously nurtured every dark and savage impulse in him. He threw his head back and laughed until tears flowed and then he began howl like the doomed animal he felt himself to be. Scratching behind the door brought him to his senses.

Vadim took the stake out and dropped the coffin back into the trunk then slammed the lid. The sound was heavy and final in the stillness. But he was not sure what to do. Every possibility seemed annihilating. And he had no idea which act would be giving in to her iron will and which constituted resistance.

While he waited, thinking, listening, Vadim spun the stake in his fingers, the tip pointing toward him, and then away. Him. Away. But he did not hesitate long. All too soon the metal door opened inward.

UV

UV wasn't a new spa, but it was new to Leila. Her best friend, her childhood girlfriend Julie, had called her about this exclusive place dedicated to youth and beauty—"Where all the glamorous people go!"—and as far as Leila could see, not one word in that conversation, at least concerning the elite aspect of *UV*, had been exaggeration.

No simple flagstone here. Expensive terra cotta Italian tiles led to a massive mahogany door imbedded into one of the red rock formations that made Sedona famous. The hot colors of the door and walk blended so perfectly with the dusty red rock that, without a sign or even a tasteful brass plaque, the building struck Leila as almost an invisible fortress, impenetrable, invulnerable. That appealed to her.

She entered a sleek hallway, glad to be out of the heat. More tiles, in pale, cooling grey, lined not just the floor but the walls and ceiling as well. The entrance turned into a corridor that spiraled down and around.

As Leila descended, the tiles darkened, the temperature dropped and the lights dimmed. Not a mirror in sight. That's unusual, she thought. Most spas confront you with how you look on the way in so the New You will look so much better on the way out.

A computer-like voice with well-modulated tones greeted her: "Welcome to *UV*. Continue along the path." With only one direction to walk, she couldn't be going the wrong way, but nothing else indicated it was the right way.

After what felt like an inordinately long trek downhill, Leila finally arrived at the end of the corridor to find a small waiting area, furnished with a plush slate couch and matching chair, the leather soft as ash, as well as a small ebony parson's table topped with smoky glass. A neat stack of the requisite magazines sat on the table. Down here the tiles were charcoal. If the light had been any dimmer, such darkness would have been unbearable.

Leila took a seat and waited. After a few moments, she picked up one of the magazines and leafed through it. The lighting was too dim to read by, which annoyed her—five years ago she could have read this print, even in this light. She refused to take out her reading glasses; she'd look at the pictures. There was the usual fare, women thin as mannikins, with large eyes, full lips, no wrinkles, and apparently no worries. A quick glance at the table told her that all of the reading matter was of the same type—what she and Julie over the last few years had taken to calling "One-Downers", because the photos always made them both feel inferior. Leila knew she was being silly. These models were a small percentage of the population, teenagers mostly, twenty years younger, so why was she comparing herself? But she also knew the answer: because she envied them and wanted to be what they were, not what she had become: ordinary. If I still had a body and face any-where near like the ones pictured in these mags, she thought, I'd be deadly!

Most of her life she'd edged out the competition. She'd always been attractive and had been blessed with a naturally good figure, bet-ter than Julie's. Their 'friendly' rivalry had been going on since high school, but Leila had always been the clear winner. And not just when it came to looks. She'd married better, produced smarter, more attrac-tive children, and had earned more money. Until five years ago. Now she was alone, stuck in a job with a glass ceiling, carrying excess weight she could not lose, using auburn 'Limage' on a monthly basis, and cursed with wrinkles that no longer disappeared after a good night's sleep.

A section of dark tiles slid apart from the rest, automatically, si-lently. The computer voice said, "Step through the opening and turn to your right."

Leila got up and entered a shadowy area. With only the subdued light from the corridor behind her, she turned right.

"Remove your clothing, then enter the room directly ahead."

She could just make out the faint outline of a doorway and a clothes horse outside it. This was certainly the most impersonal spa she'd ever been to. Still, the place had worked wonders on Julie, who was now getting things Leila had only dreamed about. Besides, Leila had paid good money to come here and, since there were no refunds, she wasn't about to bail now.

She undressed, hung up her clothes, and entered the room. Immediately a sensor light lit the doorframe, triggered no doubt by her body heat as she moved across the threshold. The tiles outside the doorframe slid shut, cutting off that dim light from the waiting area.

"Lie on the table," the voice commanded, and Leila did.

This room was small. Black floors and walls, an inky porcelain sink and matching fixtures, all ultra modern. A tall black cabinet stood near the sink which contained, she guessed, the tools the beauty expert would use to drain years from her body and face. The most peculiar item was the table. Made of midnight plastic, it was more a frame, really, with six black canvas straps stretched hammock-like across it.

She lay on the 'table', feeling vulnerable, and a bit chilly. There was no sheet with which to cover herself, and she was just about to get up and retrieve her jacket when the light surrounding the door frame went out, plunging her into utter darkness.

It was disconcerting, knowing she was lying so exposed in a room devoid of all light, located in the bowels of ancient rock. The knowledge of such density pressed in on her and her heart beat quickly. She shivered from those thoughts, and also from the cool air chilling her flesh.

Calm down! she ordered herself. You've been to spas before. She'd visited many, suffering everything, including face lifts, both surgical and non-surgical, body wraps, seaweed baths, full torso mud packs, collagen treatments, liposuction, various types of massage therapy and steam. And while the results usually produced a more or less better package than the one that had entered the salon, no spa experience had ever resulted in the rejuvenation Julie claimed.

Julie had gone in thirty pounds overweight and come out as thin as a *haute couture* model. Her cheekbones, she claimed, were prominent, the hint of jowls only a bad dream, her hips, stomach and buttocks slimmed to the point where she needed to buy a new wardrobe—"Two sizes smaller!" But it was more than just physical changes. Julie had always been timid, afraid of drawing too much attention to herself. Since coming to *UV*, she'd opened her own graphic-design studio and was already inundated with work from high-powered ad agencies. Clients had flown her to the Caribbean, and were sending her to Europe next month. She'd bought a sports car, a fur coat... And she insisted she had more men after her than she could juggle.

Leila had not been impressed. She'd been jealous! If she hadn't known Julie since childhood, she'd have thought her friend was lying. After all, going into a spa Friday and coming out on Monday...how could such a shift have occurred in body and soul in only one weekend? But Julie was a compulsive truth-teller, and Leila was here now, hoping that time would not only be slowed but reversed. She wanted her most confident self revived by the miracles promised by *UV*.

Well, 'promised' wasn't the right word. *UV* promised nothing. In fact, they did not advertise, or even produce a brochure. Their clientele was select, built strictly by word-of-mouth, with each applicant carefully screened. A friend told Julie, who told Leila, who'd had, like the others, to answer lists of personal questions and sign a legal-looking document, all by mail, to get into this exclusive salon. Of course, with the prices they charged, they didn't have to advertise—they didn't appeal to the masses, which appealed to Leila. They could afford to treat each client on an individual basis.

Leila had drastically dipped into her term deposits to come here. But if she could undergo a transformation like the one Julie experienced, something that would get her back into the flow of life with the looks and energy of a twenty-five year old, it would all be worth it. Life had been snubbing her since long before the divorce and she wanted to re-engage in a major way, by her rules. But she was honest enough with herself to realize that, at forty-something, she was no longer a valued commodity. Youth, sex-appeal, energy, aggression, they were everything, and hers had evaporated. Fifteen years of a boring marriage, three rebellious kids and a dead-end job had seen to that. But her youngest had recently left for college—hallelujah!—and Leila felt she had good years left; she wanted to spend them grabbing everything she could get her hands on. If *UV* had a way of stemming the aging process, she was all for it, whatever it was!

In the darkness she felt a presence move into the room. For some unknown reason, the skin over her backbone prickled. Why didn't that motion/heat-sensitive light go on? "Hello?" Leila said.

Without a word, what was undoubtedly a technician moved to the table and quickly strapped her in at the wrists, ankles, thighs, upper arms, and under her ribcage, then tilted the table until Leila was in an upright position. Behind, Leila heard a click, as if the cabinet door had opened. A rush of cool air hit her back. Goosebumps sprouted across her flesh and her heart beat too quickly. Why didn't the woman answer? Then the thought occurred, God, I hope it is a woman! "I've never been here before," Leila said, trying to draw the technician out, disturbed by the small voice seeping from between her own lips.

Wordlessly, something cool was tied around her eyes. What for? she wondered, since I can't see anything anyway, then realized it must be one of those gel-filled masks designed to relax the muscles surrounding the eyes.

At least it's dark, she thought; somehow she didn't want to be seen, even though this esthetician had likely labored over many bodies, some in worse shape than her own. She was about to ask the technician how she could work without light, but a sudden touch to her skin made her gasp. Her body jolted.

It was as though sharp icicles had dropped from the ceiling and pierced her stomach. But how could that be? She was upright. Obviously that was the tip of a stainless steel needle; the technician must have injected something. Then more needles on each side of both breasts. Freezing steel bit her inner elbows and wrists, the backs of her knees and ankles, her hips, her groin, her throat. She had no idea there was more than one technician in the room!

Panic rose in her chest. To distract herself from the fear creeping in, she tried to focus on what types of treatment this spa would use to remove excess water and fat from the body, severing inches from the waist, hips, thighs and buttocks, firming breasts, tightening the chin and upper arms. And she'd tried them all, it seemed. When she'd heard where *UV* was located—in the middle of Arizona, desert country—right away she'd assumed the treatments would be heat based, utilizing the natural sunlight. "The opposite," Julie confided when pressed. "They blame ultra-violet rays for skin damage, and for deforming cells and they say that leads to extra fat, water retention, and wrinkles. And all that reduces self-confidence."

"So how come they're not operating out of the North Pole?"

Julie, usually a cheerful person, had gotten testy. "Look, I don't know all the technical aspects, and I can't talk about the treatment itself. It's their big secret process—you signed the papers too! You'll just have to trust me on this: they know what they're doing. They're into anti-aging."

Cold spread across her stomach and chilled its way through her torso until it was met by the cold creeping down from her chest. Her body trembled. Iciness spread from her hips, joining what was in front and permeated her back until glacial fingernails scratched her backbone. Her body buckled uncontrollably as cold extended through her limbs. Soon she was numb from head to toe. She tried to open her mouth to ask what was going on, but found her jaw locked, leaving her only capable of guttural sounds.

Every other treatment she'd experienced had begun with heat, to open the pores and, if cold was used, it was alternating. Why were they freezing her? Her entire body had lost feeling.

This isn't bad, though, she tried to reassure herself, holding back a wave of panic. Now that the feeling had left her body, it wasn't any worse than a trip to the dentist, when the gums are frozen: no feeling, no pain. At least she hoped that was the case.

She lay in the darkness, her body corpse-like, sensing forms hovering all around, very close. There was pressure on her body, but no pain. Her heart slammed in terror. She began to feel so sleepy, dazed, as if she'd been caught in a blizzard and hypothermia had set in.

Time had no contours. Whether she was asleep or awake, dreaming, hallucinating or seeing reality, she had no idea, and that certainty ceased to matter. Images appeared on her eyelids, or was there a TV screen on the wall in front of her?—news footage of starved children; a parade of grinning skeletons, their bones rattling as they jerked along a runway in flimsy expensive costumes; red icicles hanging like stalactites, thinning to dripping points; a swarm, fluttering in the dark, a million night birds descending on prey. She felt none of this in her body, which made the tension greater.

There were many more images, all fleeting, but the one that lingered was the crimson fires of passion. Just out of reach. Like eyes that reflected her own intense hunger to devour life. She felt compelled to stare into those fires, and any desire to turn away soon vanished.

"Take a step forward."

Leila couldn't feel her limbs and was surprised when her legs moved. She walked with difficulty at first, feeling weak and dizzy. Hadn't she been strapped to the table? Her head was light and thoughts only snippets.

She still could not feel her body yet possessed energy, but the source was a mystery. She had been here—how long? Long enough. Shouldn't blood have rushed from or to her head? But it did not.

"Take six steps forward!" the voice commanded.

The voice resonated through her, like air rushing in and filling her lungs, although she could not feel herself breathing. She did as directed and passed through the doorway, which did not light up. Her eyes must have adjusted to extended darkness because it was as though she could see through a red filter. She found her clothes and dressed, aware that the blouse and slacks were far roomier than when she had removed them.

She reentered the waiting area. A small open wine bottle without a label and a crystal goblet sat on the table. The voice told her, "Quench your thirst."

She filled the glass. The earthy aroma of this beverage called out to her as she raised the glass and drank. Smoldering embers flowed through her body and suddenly burst into flame. She took on a solidity, yet was amazed by how crystal clear she felt. Renewed.

Her hand that held the glass was far slimmer. The bone on her wrist jutted out, as it had when she was younger. Smooth flesh, the color nearly translucent, the first of the age-spots gone. For a moment she imagined she could see through the skin to the blue veins below, plumped with the flowing nourishment she had just consumed.

"Proceed along the path."

As Leila moved up the spiraling corridor, feeling the air warm, watching the tiles lighten, she was aware that she, too, felt lighter. It was as though she had no body, but was a spirit, gliding, without pleasure or pain, and that the absence of both was as close to bliss as she was likely to get.

With one hand she pushed the door open. Arizona's dry cool nightair rushed in to welcome her. She stared up at the silver moon, full, sated, and breathed in its brilliance. A flock of hungry nightbirds flew across its perfect face and she felt a connection to them, as if they reflected her true nature.

The iron in the rock drew her as had the drink; she needed replenishment, and instinctively understood how to get it. What had been taken from her, she would take from others, tonight, every night.

As she headed down into the valley, she knew how to stay young, slim, beautiful and aggressive. The world belonged to her. It would come to her, and she would devour its vitality and prey on its weaknesses. Forever. After all, she was the Ultimate of her kind.

Sustenance

IT'S always hungry. In the months I've been down here, not one revolution of the planet has taken place when IT hasn't fed on me. There are no windows in this grey cell I'm locked in. Natural light cannot get through, but I know when it's night. That's when I'm tired. That's when IT comes for me.

I feel like the Marquis de Sade, writing this endless *journal diabolique* on toilet paper. With a stolen ballpoint. I hide both under the mattress. I'm not writing with the hope that this will ever be read, more to preserve whatever sanity I may have left.

I hear scratching on the wall of the next cell, gouging, really, as if a primitive tool hacks at the cement holding the cold grey bricks in place. One day enough sealer will be chiseled away and the brick will loosen sufficiently to either push out or pull inward and then...

And then all hope will be crushed. The digger will not have found a route out of this prison but only a large peephole to another cell. To me. Confined as much or even more than whoever is dismantling the wrong wall.

I used to call out. Every day. But either my voice didn't carry or else the tormented mind on the other side heard the sounds as life remembered. Or imagined I am outside this prison, my cries carried on air waves in the clean sunshine of a free world. I doubt I'll ever see that world again.

I don't bother calling now when I hear the noise. A rodent chewing through building materials. Hope digging frantically toward freedom. Toward annihilation.

Another meal has come and gone. Eating is a mundane activity. They feed me protein, meat, plenty of it, to keep up my strength no doubt. To make me last longer.

I was brought here one hot summer night when I'd had too much white wine and was feeling maudlin enough to foolishly wander down an alley off a side street. I remember seeing the man, or what I thought of then as a man, lingering ahead in the shadows. My affair with Alan was over for good this time. I felt reckless. Sentimentally vulnerable. Drunk. And then...

I awoke in this stark box, blazing with light so bright it kills any tones of color that might exist. Empty white everywhere—the bed, the floor and walls, the toilet, the plastic chair and table.

A matron in nurse's whites came first. She wouldn't answer questions but made a silent and, over days, steady demand that the medical history chart and menu card be ticked off. At first I refused. She wouldn't give, neither would I. But charred meat was slipped through the small opening in the door, meat only, except for a glass of orange juice, on a time schedule that seems to be about twice each night. I'm not as strong as she is. I got hungry. I gave in.

Eventually I filled out the menu card—the only one—but since then still nothing arrives but meat. At least the cut is choice and cooked medium, not too bloody, not too 'done', the way I like it, although I was never much of a meat eater. There's something to survival of the fittest. The other reason I capitulated was the feeling of devastating weakness that hit from the first time IT began to feed.

The ritual is the same nightly. The lights are dimmed until blackness swallows the room and everything in it. I hear metal slide against metal as the door is unbolted from the outside. Through thick darkness I can just barely make out a form gliding into the room, bringing with it brittle cold. More than seeing, I sense IT wafting toward me like a gust of Arctic air. The air seems to form ice crystals as though molecular movement has slowed. At first I could not identify the unpleasant odor. Now I recognize the stench. Flesh. Rotting. The putrefaction of death overwhelming life.

The thing that comes for me has red eyes that glow like tail lights on a pitch black highway. I back up against the wall to the next cell, which stops me dead, and cringe there. Something about those glowing crimson coals, the way they throb, or pulse reminds me of flies swarming over spoiled beef... I can't remember more.

The eyes, the rank smell, the bone-splitting cold overwhelm me. Those parts become greater than the sum of my whole. That's all I know until suddenly the lights are blinding and I'm prone on the floor, the side of my throat scorched. There's always a plastic pitcher and glass on the table. When I sit up I'm dizzy and nauseous so eventually I sip water and pat wetness against the searing wound on my neck. My fingers always touch blood.

IT comes once in what feels like a twenty-four hour cycle. After the first session I felt so weak my body seemed to have only air inside, a balloon on the verge of becoming deflated. I knew I was dying and made a decision to eat the meat and drink the juice and exercise and do whatever I could to help myself. When I filled out the menu card I stole the pen. I don't know what I'll do when it runs out of ink.

The worse part is the loneliness. There are moments when I disappear. Not physically but I go somewhere inside and a lot of time passes and when I return to this prison I don't know where I've been, only that it's better than here. I find that frightening.

I've always been what they call an extrovert—being with people recharges me. That's one of the problems Alan and I had. He's an introvert. Insisted on being alone more than our relationship could sustain. But that's all over, and now I wish I was more like him.

Since my first week of captivity in this 'laboratory', the nurse has come back only four times, to take my blood pressure, blood samples, check my heart and other vital organs. She still says nothing but at least I can observe her now that my initial confused terror has subsided. She's tiny, greying, all efficiency, focused on her duties like a cyborg some master race built to fulfil one function only. I talk to her, ask her questions, but she never responds and won't meet my eye, although I've seen that hers are grey and piercing. I kicked over the chair once when her back was turned. She jerked. I know she can hear. It was a small victory.

The monster that drains my blood is another story. Nightly he—I don't know why but I've started thinking of IT as male—comes in the same way, does the same things to me. I can't stay conscious. I've tried avoiding contact with those bloody irises but it's impossible. Once I talked to him, IT, to plead really, but the room went sub-zero and I heard a hiss like air being let out of a radiator, and that's all I remember.

It wasn't that long ago I would have said there was nothing worse than the horror of being raped nightly. I was wrong. A new feeling has developed that terrifies me. Anticipation. When I hear the metal scraping and feel the chill sliding in as the door opens—this is hard to write—I find I'm looking forward to him, IT, somehow. IT relieves the soul-crushing boredom, even for a little while, and I know I'll be dead to this isolated world for precious minutes. This is all so twisted and masochistic I don't want to think about it. I worry about my sanity.

The only other distraction to endless time under white glare is the scratching. The hours I'm awake the noise is incessant, but I welcome it. I imagine someone like myself on the other side—I've even named her—Lisa. Lisa is more determined than I am. Inspiring. So much so that for the last week I've been using the spoon they send in with the pre-cut meat to dig from my side. Something in the sound of both of us trying, struggling, has renewed my hope, even though I know deep down that in the end we'll only find each other and not a way out. But it's something to do. Something to look forward to. Something more positive than welcoming IT.

Something has happened that frightens me. Food doesn't come anymore. At least three twenty-four hour periods have gone by and, nothing. Not the nurse, not the food. Just IT.

I've been alone with the scrapings. If I hadn't given back the spoon I'd help. I don't want to damage my pen and there's nothing else I can use. Lisa's efforts lift the weight of despair pressing in on me, and yet that's stupid. Lisa will get through, and soon. I can feel it. Unless she starves to death first. Or I do. And then what? But I feed the insane plans within me. Together we can find a way out of here, I'm convinced of it. We can fight IT off—two are certainly stronger than one. At least one of us can stay awake when he, IT, feeds and that might lead to a way of killing IT. Maybe she has more tools. With her for company, I would sacrifice my pen and put it to better use—it could be a weapon. At the very least, together we can dig through the wall to the outside and...

A small chink falls through on my side. I run to the wall. The hole is the size of an iris. I peer through and it is dark. Then bright light.

She must be looking at me as I am looking at her. I press my lips to the hole. "I can't help you. Keep digging, Lisa," I say, then realize that Lisa may not be her name. She may not even be female. "Keep digging," I repeat, and feel compelled to add "Lisa," sure she'll understand when I explain.

I am so excited I can't keep still. Despite my resolve, I use the other end of my pen to try to loosen some of the mortar from my side. I work for a long time, building up a sweat, shattering the plastic, feeling weak from hunger and long-term blood loss, but I finally pry out a small chunk and feel extremely proud of myself.

I carry on as long as I can until I drop from exhaustion. "I'm going to take a nap," I say into the hole, now forehead size and shape. Lisa looks through again at the same time as I do. I back away to let light in, but the brick is so thick she's all shadows and my eyes are blurring anyway. "I'll be back," I assure her. "Sleep will make me stronger."

When I awake the hole is the size of a human head. I push my face against it and call "Hello!" There is no response from the other side. I feel panicked. Maybe she's asleep. Or, dead, the gloomy part of me thinks. No, I refuse to accept that.

The hole is large enough that I can pick up the plastic chair and use the leg as a hammer. It's awkward but better than nothing. I pound at an angle and large chunks of weakened cement come away from the edges. After a long time I have a space big enough to get my head and shoulders through.

The room on the other side is just like mine. On the bed, back to me, is a form under the blanket. "Wake up!" I call out. "Please. Lisa, don't leave me." She does not stir. The dread crawling up my body deflates me. I cannot bear the idea that I am completely alone here.

I crawl to my bed and jot these notes before IT comes.

Sounds wake me. I feel delirious. Light-headed. Beyond hunger. Sick from despair. I look across at the hole. It is now large enough to crawl through. I hear familiar noises and they coalesce into the hopeful sound of someone breaking through the wall. Lisa!

I rush to the opening and look through. I see legs and a white skirt, similar to the white hospital gown the nurse gave me to wear. Yes, she is female. I knew it! I feel overwhelmed with joy and sadness and great tears gush out of me along with a string of anguished wails. She stops working. I see her bend down and I stand up and step back from the wall so she can get through.

Whatever happens, I think, I will not be alone. There's some comfort in that. No, for me that is all comfort.

I see her small hands and the top of her head, cement dust sprinkled liberally over her hair. I reach out to help her but freeze. Something is familiar but my mind just will not make the connection. She lifts her face as she emerges from the womb and glares at me. Blank grey eyes, piercing. Robot-like efficiency. Nurses's whites. Fierce hunger. Scalpel raised as a weapon.

I have learned to like my meat very rare, or *tartare*, as de Sade would say. It gives me more energy. This can be messy; pools of slippery blood streak the floors, but that can't be helped. We cope.

Now that my quarters have doubled in size and, thanks to Lisa there are two new pens and extra rolls of toilet paper, I have more room for my writings, which I no longer hide.

Thank God Lisa is still with me, although she sits in the corner most of the time, not moving, not speaking. She is not the lively companion I envisioned. Still, I value her company. There's someone to talk to. I've taken over her room, and she's in mine. A change is as good as a rest, I tell her patiently, but she only stares at me as though I'm crazy.

Time has lost its grip on me, which is another benefit to having a friend. But Lisa is so tiny, I fear for her at times. She seems to be wasting away before my eyes. It's as though every day there's a bit less of her. And what's left stinks. Lisa refuses to bathe and I've washed her down occasionally but the effect is temporary.

Sometimes I get mad and tell her I don't think she's helping herself at all, but then she's not really as strong as I am, either physically or emotionally, and I've had to accept her limitations as well as my strengths. Nor is she the tower of optimism and energy I imagined. Still, if she hadn't dug through the tunnel, we wouldn't be together. HE wouldn't be satisfied. And, after all, we are here to sate HIM. I understand now. Lisa taught me that. I look forward to HIS visits. I sustain HIM heart and soul, just as Lisa nourishes me.

The lights are dimming. We must prepare. All three of us. Giving and receiving are sacred responsibilities. The nadir of our days, the apex of our nights. I must hurry. Dinner is about to be served.

I Am No Longer

I am not the same woman I used to be. Events alter all of us. Sometimes irrevocably.

This journal began the day they delivered the computer. It's been a slow agonizing process, practicing for hours, hitting the modified keyboard with a touch stick clamped between my teeth. The spot where my jaw is hinged still aches much of the time, as do the muscles at the side of my neck, but I've got the hang of it. Those areas of my body are strong.

The computer is essential. It's vital that I write everything down. Somebody has got to keep a record; I have to keep a record. For now I have nothing else to do.

I never dreamed I'd end up in a place like Dry Plains. On the other hand, no nightmare ever warned I'd be paralyzed from C-7, the seventh vertebra down, my voice box severed in the six-car pileup outside Houston. That the newly conceived fetus inside me would be miscarried. That I'd spend the rest of my life talking to myself and what's left of the world through modern technology, the same technology that used to confuse and annoy me. But then I've come to understand and accept many things recently. I'm not the person I was.

By the time the hospital sent me home, the bills had piled to the ceiling and Terry was at his wit's end. The recession hit the factory where he was a manager. Recent trade agreements had taken a lot of work to Mexico. The baggage handler job in Dry Plains was all he could find. At least the bungalow near the airport was cheap.

Terry's life insurance paid off the mortgage. And bought the computer. I need the computer to keep Terry's truth alive. He knew what was going on at the airport. About all the 'accidents.' The flights where more passengers disembarked than the plane held. About the Indians. I'm one-quarter Comanche myself. On my mother's side. Maybe that's why I believed him. Now I believe him for other reasons.

I had a premonition of Terry's death. I get feelings. Always have. Like my grandmother. My vision blurs, I hear echoes. Sometimes a headache slices into the middle of my brain. Before the accident, my backbone used to feel as if someone had rammed an icy steel rod down it.

I tried to tell him: don't go, you're in danger. Back then I only had the letter board and pointer to spell out a warning. It was tedious, I was always frustrated, the stick in my mouth, fumbling to point to the right letters, Terry having to figure out the words and then make sentences. He was endlessly patient, but that night he was late for work. He only got half the message: 'Don't go!'

He paused at the door in his midnight-blue coveralls and looked at me with eyes brown as fertile soil that always reminded me of the harvest back on my grandmother's farm when I was a girl. Of plenty. Of happier times. What I couldn't say with words, I told him with my eyes. His turned fearful. "Got to go, Meg," he said, covering it up with forced cheerfulness. He kissed my mouth with his generous lips and smiled, his teeth so white, one chipped. The scent of musk from his aftershave lingered. "*Rosanne's* on tonight. Why don't you watch it?" The door closed. I remember the cold empty feeling in the house; I swear I felt that rod up my spine.

His kiss left an invisible imprint on my lips; it caressed my skin through half the night, that and the tears coating my cheeks.

It was late when the world exploded. Even the dead must have felt the bomb tear up the runway. It was as if the earth had been slashed to the core. Hell fire shot skyward until the flames licked heaven's gate. The house grew frigid. I knew the moment Terry left the earth; the scent of musk vanished. His body was never found. That night I changed again.

Soon I started seeing them. Before they'd been just rumors. Talk Terry brought home from the airport. He didn't tell me, of course. He wouldn't have wanted to frighten me. I overheard him talking to his buddies. About the passenger who died of a sudden heart attack and then, two hours later, got up and walked, shoe soles not making a sound as they contacted the floor, skin too grey and mottled to be called living. About the red-headed Mexican twins, children really. They followed a black woman and her daughter from Atlanta into the washroom. And never came out. Two bodies were found, one adult, one teenage, the skin stripped off the way a hunter peels the hide from his prey to get at the carcass. Stories about hideous babies with yellow eyes and red teeth, who resembled stone demons, who sucked blood from engorged nipples. About half a dozen old men who carried tomahawks into the smoke shop, hacked the attendant to pieces, scattered tobacco all over the tarmac... And all the while it was business as usual at the airport.

I heard the stories and believed them. And now I see the spirits myself. Just like my grandmother used to. All day and all night. They roam the fields surrounding the airport, passing the house. One paid me a visit. That's how I know they're ancestors. And how I know they are not wholesome spirits. They aren't here to help but to punish. For deeds long forgotten. To exact revenge on the sons of the fathers, and their sons. And the mothers and their daughters.

"I am Tacomaak." He said that without opening his mouth, our brains like two modems, connected. There was something hollow-looking about him yet sturdy. He was solid enough to break down the door all by himself but he could walk through walls, which I suspect is how he got inside my house. Maybe, in the past, I'd have been scared. But that part of me dried up and blew away with the parched earth of this desolate place. In my new widow's grief, I transmitted the message: Why are you here? Why now?

He was two heads shorter than me when I'd been able to stand. Dirty skin and hair, prominent nose and cheekbones slick with sweat stinking of mesquite. Maniacal black eyes glared through me, reflecting distorted images from the spirit land he came from. He knew I was paralyzed but I doubt he'd have found me a threat even if I could defend myself. From the way he stood rooted to the earth, I knew he didn't feel threatened by anyone. Right away I sensed he was Comanche, although I can't say how I knew that. My mother did not like to talk about our native blood. I've seen movies, though. He was dressed warrior- fashion, fierce ochre and red clay face-paint, natural leather headband, a tomahawk and stone knife hanging from a beaded belt decorated with what I believe were scalps. Thick swatches of hair dangled in a row, shades of brown. One blonde. Like Terry's. Dried blood clinging to it. Staring at those bloody strands and then into Tacomaak's eyes, suddenly I understood everything. The bomb had not killed Terry. I knew why he had come here.

Any dry dust motes of emotion that remained in me were moistened by my tears. They quickly turned into a mud slide that swallowed me. I never would have imagined myself pleading, but I did, in thought. He showed no mercy. His sharp knife gouged deep into my chest over my heart. It was not a wound that leads to death but a calculated mutilation of pure savagery. His mouth clamped onto my breast. Physically I could not feel his obscene kiss, or the brutal rape of my disabled body that followed—for that I am grateful to any benevolent spirits who may still exist. But physical pain is not the worst kind. Loaded into my cellular memory banks was an image. For a second two faces superimposed one over the other. A glitch. Mesquite and musk clogged my nostrils. I became irreversibly numb.

Generous lips smile. White teeth, one chipped. Smeared with red gore. Blazing hatred in inhuman eyes scorches me. He despises my mixed blood even as he greedily steals it.

I am not the same woman. I cannot feel the twisted thing growing inside me but I sense its coiled, warped energy draining my life force. My existence is a flat computer graphic. RAM memories keep me alive: a blond man who loved me with all his heart; my grandmother who blessed me. I am driven. I must delete something. If I do not, who will?

When the reincarnated demon crawls from my womb like a maggot, I will drive the plastic touch stick I have sharpened into its callous heart. And if I fail, if my body expires as this malevolent being seizes life, you who read this must act.

Do not be fooled—the spawn is not human. It is no friendly ancestor returning to guide us in our time of great need. It has come to destroy us. All of us.

Kill it!

I write this easily and with absolute certainty. The word mercy is not in my program.

I am no longer the person I once was.

Leesville, Louisiana

---

*Ronee Sue stands at the gray tentflap, half-in, half-out, trembling.
Malaleik, The Dream Catcher, is a blinding light lurking behind the low
white screen. A townie, female, always a female, sits in the chair. She lets
The Dream Catcher hold her hand. Cold sweat slides down from Ronee
Sue's armpits and from under her breasts. Her heart hollers in her chest and
her legs feel planted in the earth. She wets her lips, ready to warn the girl, but
hesitates. Her job is clearing lots, setting up tents, selling tickets, cleaning
stalls, whatever's useful. If Nolan, or Mr. Peabody or, God forbid,
Ozymandias Prather catches her interfering with business... She calls out
anyway·"Don't give away your dreams!" but her words are ignored. Each
night the girls are different but the same. Young, vulnerable, full of hopes for
the future, hopes that will erode just from living. They shell out to have their
narrow lives expanded with false promises.*

*The Dream Catcher listens patiently, a freak therapist feeding the girl
what she longs to hear. Suddenly Malaleik rises. The Dream Catcher has
grown large. In the belly. The girl too stands up, but slowly. Her husband
catches her hand. The two turn. They walk toward Ronee Sue. The young
thing smiles, but her eyes are icicles. The warmth that should be there has
been sucked out. She looks like hard winter....*

Ronee Sue burst through her trailer door. She staggered down the
metal steps into a blazing mid-day sun, grateful for the searing light. It
burned away the nightmare images and snapped her back to the reality
of the camp grounds.

Shit, another scorcher, Ronee Sue thought. Way too hot for May.

The oppressive heat began prickling her skin. She raked her fingers through her short dark hair and looked around. The last two times Ronee Sue Baines crossed the country—by thumb—she'd been unlucky enough to get stuck right here, in this swamp some demented visionary had named after General Lee. She favored warm weather, but 100-plus degrees was pushing it. Yesterday, while clearing the lot for the freak tent, she'd accidently stepped on a dead coral snake, except it wasn't dead, just too heat-exhausted to slither away. At least the show would be out of this pit day after tomorrow.

"Hot one, Mr. Peabody."

The easygoing man nodded in passing. He looked tired and older but she wrote it off to the humidity.

"Makes for business," he said. "Folks swelter all day, come nightfall they crave excitement. That's us."

Ronee Sue took a deep breath of thick, heavy air; it was like trying to inhale hot water. A childhood terror of suffocation seized her. She thought about returning to the cooler comfort of the trailer, but that was where the nightmare lurked. Instead she dragged herself across the patched dirt to the cook tent. By the time she got there her pale blue *Lifestyles of the Broke and Obscure* T-shirt was splotched with sweat.

Malaleik, The Dream Catcher, sat at the only table with a vacant seat, and Ronee Sue hesitated. If that empty chair was next to a performer, or even one of the other creepy freaks, she wouldn't have thought twice. But Malaleik rattled her. White hair and bleached skin, born without finger- or toenails, in Ronee Sue's opinion there was something, well, lacking. And those unearthly eyes. Colorless. When they locked on, it was like being stared at by a husky, only worse--they made Ronee Sue feel like she was buried in snow, trapped under packed ice, freezing to death. Suddenly the heat felt just fine.

She grabbed a cup of coffee and a slice of soggy toast from the steam table then squeezed onto the edge of the picnic table bench directly across from Malaleik, who had been watching her. Ronee Sue smiled quickly, careful to turn away.

"Another dream?" The freak's voice was permafrost.

"How'd you know?"

"I'm The Dream Catcher. It's my job." Malaleik sipped iced lemonade. In the month since Ronee Sue joined the show in Florida, she had yet to see Malaleik eat food. She did not even know if The Dream

Catcher was a man or a woman. Most people said "he," but Ronee Sue wasn't so sure. Especially lately, since she'd noticed the swells beneath that blousy shirt and fuller hips stretching the white pleated pants. Of course, Malaleik had gained weight. A lot. Most of it in the belly. Once skeletal, The Dream Catcher must have loaded on thirty pounds in half as many days. Ever since ...well, ever since Ronee Sue's nightmares began.

"Give me your dream and the terror will evaporate. Money-back guarantee."

Ronee Sue shook her head. "Can't remember." She swallowed coffee and munched toast. No way would she reveal the repetitive nightmare, especially because it was Malaleik who made the dream scary.

"You'll come to trust me." Glacial fingers touched Ronee Sue's bare forearm. Frozen metal sticking to human flesh. The chill penetrated. Skin. Muscle. It struck bone. Ronee Sue jerked her arm free. Their eyes met. She felt like she was falling. Empty whiteness caused her head to hurt. She wanted to sleep...

"Hey! First-of-May!" She didn't have to look up to know who was putting her down by calling her a newcomer. Still, she grabbed the opportunity. "Help Okie hose the bulls. And clean the turds."

Nolan always assigned her the worst jobs. She liked the elephants, and cooling them down was okay. But burying their mounds of stinking shit was bad news, especially in this heat. She was hired as an all-around helper, a job men usually do. Being new to circus life didn't help.

"Sure," she said, standing. Her appetite had faded and this seemed like a good chance to escape. From both of them.

She'd nearly made it out of the mess when Nolan yelled, "Tonight you're on sideshow, front door."

"Why me again?" she grumbled.

"Peabody's orders. Seems Malaleik, here, likes your company."

Malaleik, The Dream Catcher, stood. Ronee Sue watched that bloated stomach sway toward her and stop. A cold voice whispered in her ear, "Would you like to join me in my trailer?"

The chortles and macho wit from nearby tables chased Ronee Sue out the door.

By five-thirty Ronee Sue was beat. She had half an hour to duck in the trailer she shared with Clara the Clown and Mitzi, a contortionist who'd joined up last week, both of whom resented bunking with a non performer. She took a quick bucket bath and changed her clothes. Zipping up her jeans, Ronee Sue wondered what sorry sense of adventure had compelled her to sign on with this mud show. There were easier ways to travel.

But she had signed on and she was a sticker. The show would take her out west and eventually up north where she'd spend part of the summer with her dad in Chicago before heading back to Orlando for the winter to see her mom.

Her mom. She could still hear the warnings. Everything from "Don't go gettin' yourself knocked up," to "Flittin' around the country all the time. You ain't livin' in the real world." Hell, if reality meant ending up like her mom--seven babies in as many years, and alone to boot--Ronee Sue would pass. Twenty-five still left plenty of years to settle down and have kids. If she was living in a dreamworld, she wasn't about to part with it yet.

Her cot looked comfy. A nap would do the trick. But she had to be at the sideshow. Now. And then there was the nightmare. Lying in wait. Hungry. Burning away at her soul like dry ice chewing through skin. Every damn time she shut her eyes.

She took a breath of close air and headed out.

All Ronee Sue had to do was stand inside the flap at the entrance and collect tickets. It wasn't hard work. But everybody in their right mind hated this job. Nobody could stomach being close to the freaks for long.

Inside the tent the air was wicked with stink and moisture. She tied the canvas flap back; oily grit. There was something eerie about this night. As the sun sank, the heat rose. She opened another button on her plaid shirt.

It was early and there were few townies for the barker to catch. But two kids peeked in. Both still teenagers, blond and painfully wide-eyed. The girl was very pregnant--her gold wedding band sinking into a puffy finger. The reedy husband grinned—he had a tooth missing, bottom front—and nodded, then handed over the tickets.

They looked around the dimly-lit tent, confused, sweatings, a bit scared. "Just wander through," Ronee Sue mother-henned them.

Carmella sat closest to the flap. Her third eye put a lot of people off. When the psychic winked, the future momma's face paled. Ronee Sue watched a look pass between the couple. They changed direction pronto and headed for Gore, whose mounds of flab seemed ready to burst the plate glass wall he sat behind. They looked revolted. And it got worse.

Mr. Tane. Mother Goose. Haman. Lance. The whole weird tour. And Ronee Sue knew just how those two kids felt. Here it was, weeks later, and she still wanted to puke or run screaming from these freaks. It wasn't so much the physical deformities that bothered her. They gave off a kind of diseased energy that sucked in everybody who came near.

Finally young Mr. and Mrs. Leesville got to Malaleik. "Listen, hon." The girl—it was always the females who noticed— read the sign tacked to the low white screen: GIVE ME YOUR DREAMS.

Hubby, sweat dripping off his nose, wanted out but the Mrs. plunked herself onto the chair. Malaleik, hidden by the screen from the collar-bone down, cool and rigid as an iceberg, smiled that Arctic smile and took the girl's hand. And Ronee Sue shivered.

Suddenly she remembered. The nightmare. Every night. A mirror of freak show reality. The other players changed, but not she nor Malaleik. The terrifying dream, she now knew, was trying to tell her something. To warn her.

The way The Dream Catcher listened to the dream reminded her of a swamp sucker feeding on blood. And when it was over, that girl looked empty. Stone cold. Just like all the others before her.

As Ronee Sue watched the couple leave the tent, she realized some-thing was different. She turned. The Dream Catcher stood. Their eyes locked for a moment then Ronee Sue looked down and gasped. Malaleik was skinny again. Bone thin. No belly. A skeleton, grinning, frozen in time.

It tore at her all through the shift. How could somebody shrink like that in just a few hours? She covered the possibilities but only one made any sense. The Dream Catcher was pregnant. And had a miscar-riage. Or an abortion. There was no other answer.

As business picked up, the intense heat weighed on Ronee Sue's head. She couldn't breathe and things looked hazy around the edges. Her thoughts darkened. By ten o'clock, when Joey took over for her,

Ronee Sue had herself convinced that Malaleik had done something nasty.

It was too hot to eat and a cool drink didn't help. The air felt like solid fire when she took it in. She moved fast through the backyard behind the big top. Nobody saw her slip into The Dream Catcher's trailer.

She turned on the light and looked around. The place was stark, colorless, odorless. A bunk was made up with white sheets. There were empty white cupboards. The small space looked unlived in.

The real oddity was the full-size freezer running off propane. Next to it, stacked neat as could be, were a dozen black boxes. She picked one up—it was stone, maybe eight inches square—and lifted the lid. Empty.

Ronee Sue didn't know what devil had caused her to sneak in here. There was no dead baby on the bed, no fetus floating in a pail of blood. Maybe the heat was frying her brain. She'd better hightail it before she got caught. Just a peek in that freezer, then I'm on my way, she thought.

"Oh, God." She sighed. Cold white puffs wafted out. She leaned into the relief. As the cloud evaporated she saw another onyx box. She reached in and lifted it out. Icy cold zipped through thc nerves of her fingertips and up her hand.

She lid was stuck and she tapped it open. Nothing but frozen water. A big gray ice cube.

She was closing the box when she thought she saw movement. Ice is solid, she reminded herself. But there it was. Squiggling. A flat dark form? A thin white shadow? A tadpole maybe, half a foot long. She squinted and looked closer. Nothing. I'm losing it, she thought, but then had a brainstorm.

Ronee Sue went to the Coleman and moved the coffeepot so she could put the box on the grill. In seconds a blue-yellow flame rushed up to meet the bottom. She kept the lid off the box to watch the contents melt.

The form seemed to twitch. As ice liquified, whatever was in there jerked like an animal caught in a trap trying to free itself.

Black and white blurred. A frosty rainbow buckled and swirled in the center and rippled away. Shards of light stabbed her eyes and penetrated her brain. Ronee Sue screamed. Everything went black. Then gold beetles with silvered backs, millions of them, scurried toward her, biting through her eyelids. She panicked and tripped. As she fell, she smacked the side of her head on the floor, hard enough to burst an eardrum. Pain streaked through her head and the insects faded into sparkling, glittenng, crystalline stars. They pulsed against a colorless background until the sky fragmented, so fast it made her hyperventilate. By the time she got her breath right, she wished she hadn't. The reek of sickeningly sweet cedar and honey, a stink like tar and putrid skunk filled the room. Overpowering stenches of life and death washed her cells. Air–light–sound–smell–form throbbed and raged. Objects flew every which way. And people long dead, plus ones she prayed had never lived, paraded past. Monstrous creatures chewed her flesh, slurped her blood. Punishing voices. And beneath it all a rumble like the fury of an earthquake, or too many bad dreams.

The room went subzero and Ronee Sue shook until her muscles locked in understanding: These were all the dreams that Malaleik had stolen. No human being was meant to experience this.

Blind, half-deaf, she struggled to her feet. Primordial energy, ooz-ing with violence, erupted. Frigid tentacles seized her. Frostbite stran-gled her cries. She felt snow-bound, buried under impacting ice.

And then she heard The Dream Catcher. An avalanche. She plummeted through glacial space, grateful to be losing feeling, getting sleepy, melding with a great inhuman nothingness.

"Give me your dream!" Malaleik demanded.

And Ronee Sue did.

PHOTO BY HUGUES LEBLANC

About Nancy Kilpatrick

Nancy Kilpatrick has been called Canada's Queen of the Undead. She has been likened to Anne Rice, although most of her fiction is set in the here-and-now and much of it is set in Canada.

Nancy moved to Canada from the United States in the 1970s and has lived in Toronto, Vancouver and Montreal. She returned to Montreal three years ago and lives there with her black cat Bella. She travels, visiting cemeteries around the world with her companion, photographer Hugues Leblanc.

Much of her work involves the vampire. She has published thirteen novels, and those focused on the undead are: *Reborn*; *Near Death*; *Child of the Night* (the *Power of the Blood* trilogy); *Dracul–an Eternal Love Story* (based on the musical); *As One Dead* (set in the role-playing world *Vampire: The Masquerade*); *The Darker Passions: Dracula*; *The Darker Passions: Carmilla* (the last two written under the nom de plume Amarantha Knight). She also edited seven anthologies, one a collection of erotic vampire stories, *Love Bites*. Over half of her short fiction concerns vampires, and she has published two books of vampire novellas, *Sex and the Single Vampire* and *Endorphins*. She has also written four issues for the *VampErotica* comic series. Nancy works as an editor as well as a writer, and has edited two anthologies for Ace Books, *In the Shadow of the Gargoyle*; and *Graven Images* (October 2000). She has also edited five anthologies of erotic horror under her pen name.

Nancy publishes horror, dark fantasy, erotica and mysteries. She has been a finalist four times for the Bram Stoker award, a finalist five times for the Aurora Award, and in 1992 she won the Arthur Ellis Award, best short story for her story *Mantrap*.

Having written so much on the subject of vampires, Nancy has been a popular guest at conventions and with the media. She wrote the article "Archetypes and Fearful Allure" for the *Writer's Digest* book *Writing Horror and Dark Fantasy.* She taught writing at George Brown College for 10 years, and now teaches courses on the internet for two schools and does private courses including, Writing Vampire Fiction.

Look for Nancy's work in other books by Mosaic Press:

Northern Frights 1
Northern Frights 2
Northern Frights 3
Northern Frights 4
Northern Frights 5
Cold Blood 5
The Best of Cold Blood

Visit Nancy's website at:

www.sff.net/people/nancyk